I put in another batch of coins and dialed. Of course, I could get his wife. I found myself wishing she'd answer, and in just what insinuating, damaging way I'd speak to her.

But it was Alan who said, "Hello?"

I took a deep breath. "I just called to tell you what a bastard I think you are. You raped me and got me pregnant, and I'm here desperately trying to make sure that my baby's all right and it's all because of you!"

"What the—Claudia?"

"Yes, me, Claudia . . ."

THE
SEARCH

Isabelle Holland

FAWCETT JUNIPER • NEW YORK

A Fawcett Juniper Book
Published by Ballantine Books
Copyright © 1991 by Isabelle Holland

Library of Congress Catalog Card Number: 91-91819

ISBN 0-449-70342-8

Manufactured in the United States of America

First Edition: May 1991

THE SEARCH

— 1 —

The fear started slowly. It was nothing more than an item in the paper on a back page. And I wouldn't have noticed it because I usually don't read even our town's paper, except that day Mr. O'Shea, our history teacher, decided it was time for us to start keeping up with current events.

"You'll notice that I've put a well-known metropolitan daily on your desks this morning. We've been talking about the world of the past two centuries. Now we're going to look at the results of all that history as it is today. So read the headline first, because it's obviously meant to scream at you—"

It was interesting. History's one of my favorite subjects (along with art and English), and in the school I go to it's called that—not social studies or civics. I think that's why my aunt and uncle pushed my parents into sending me there. "It's a little old-fashioned, I'll admit," Uncle James said. "But at least she'll come out knowing where Africa and Australia are, which is more than I can say for most of the kids around here."

Since Uncle James teaches at a university not far from here, what he said had a lot of influence. So when Mother and Dad went abroad for Dad to take up his embassy post and for Mother to do her research in international law, I came to live in Bainsbridge with Uncle James and Aunt Mary and started going to St. Albans School, a private coed high school where Uncle James came as a guest lecturer every now and then. I'd been there about a month when Mr. O'Shea brought in the newspapers.

"Okay," he said when the bell sounded. "Take the newspapers home and write a short essay for me on what you think is the most significant and/or interesting item in it." Mr. O'Shea was big on essays, which was fine with me, because I like to write.

As we were leaving he called to me. "Claudia, could you come here a minute?"

Joe and Debbie gave me an odd look as I turned. Part of me wished he hadn't spoken. St. Albans was the third school I'd attended in two years, and because I'd lost most of one year, I was older than some of the others in class. They were sixteen. I was already seventeen. If I just hadn't lost that year, I'd have been younger than most in the class, which was what I'd always been in school up to two years ago—younger and getting all A's. But it wasn't any use thinking about that now.

"Yes, Mr. O'Shea?" I said, approaching his desk.

He smiled. "You write well. I'm sure your English teacher's told you that. I hope you keep on with it."

I made myself smile back, trying very hard to remember that he was only meaning to be helpful. But it was as though recent memories reached out and laid a cold hand on me.

Mr. O'Shea stopped smiling. "Are you all right?" he asked.

"Fine," I said, willing it to be true. "Thanks for—for

2

saying . . . saying what you did." I was backing away as I said this, then I said "Good-bye," and ran down the hall after the others.

"I think he has a thing for you," Debbie said.

"No," I said. I must have spoken more violently than I meant to, because Debbie, who was opening up her locker, stared.

"I was only kidding, for Pete's sake," she said.

"Yeah, I know," I made myself smile. It used to be so easy for me to get along with people, especially kids my own age. Now it was hard.

"You look tired," Aunt Mary commented when I got home that afternoon. She was kneeling in front of the flower bed right under the windows, trowel in hand.

I paused and stared. "It's practically winter," I said. "So what can you be planting?"

"It's known as preparing the soil." She looked up and smiled. "You look more like your father every day."

"But not his nose," I said, kidding. My father has a very good nose for a man, large and aquiline, but it wouldn't look good on a woman.

"A much smaller version. Don't worry, it's very nice. By the way, James has decided that he's going to take us to that new Italian restaurant in the mall for dinner tonight."

I knew they were trying to be hospitable. "That sounds like fun," I said, and went inside the house and up to my room.

There were times when I wished they knew what had happened to me in the past year and a half. If they did, they might stop trying to "draw me out." But Mother and Father were adamant: No one must know. So people like my uncle and aunt who had known me before when they

3

visited us both abroad and at home were left puzzled. The girl who had been outgoing and friendly and chatty to the point where periodically someone—usually Mother or Father or often one of my teachers—would say in joking exasperation, "Why don't you just shut up and listen sometimes?" had become withdrawn and rather silent. I knew it and tried to get back my liking for and fascination with people. But too much had happened. Some vital bridge had been destroyed. The psychologist at the hospital had told me that after a while I'd get back to normal. But I didn't really believe him. Maybe it was because I didn't want to.

When I got upstairs, I found Samantha, my Himalayan cat, curled up on my bed, her fuzzy stomach showing its Siamese colors. Himalayan is simply long-haired Siamese. I had brought her with me from home, and lived in mortal fear that she'd get out and be run over in the street in front of the house. So I was always very careful to keep her in my room and kept the door shut when I was out. Before, my parents and I lived in apartments in Washington and New York and there was no question of her going out.

"Hi, Sammy," I said, sitting down beside her. I started rubbing her tummy. A loud purr rattled from her throat. Under my hand I could feel her whole body vibrate. After a few minutes I lay down beside her and put my face against her back. "Mmmm," I said. It was strange, I thought. I'd never been an animal person before. Now I liked animals better than I did people.

It was when we were in the middle of our pasta at the restaurant in the mall that a tall man and a pleasant-looking woman walked up. "No, don't get up, James," the man said as my uncle started to rise. "We just came over to say hello. How are you?" he said to Aunt Mary.

"Fine," Aunt Mary said, smiling. "And how's the new addition?"

The woman grinned. "It's unbelievable that a seven-pound blob could wreak so much havoc in what used to be a civilized household."

"It's not unbelievable at all," the man said, "when you count in the fact that that same blob keeps us up most of the night."

"Andy and Margaret have a brand new baby," Aunt Mary said to me.

They seemed awfully old, I thought, to have a new baby, except that I knew, theoretically, that women could have babies into their forties and fifties. All that had been explained to me once. Andy and Margaret looked to be my uncle and aunt's age, the mid-forties. Uncle James was my father's older brother and he and Aunt Mary had never had any children.

"How nice," I said. "Congratulations!" And hoped the words came out as bland and innocuous as I wanted them to be.

The woman made a face. "We're a little late getting started, but, I suppose, better late than never."

I looked down at my plate, willing them to go away. I didn't want to be part of aimless, pointless chatter about their baby.

Eventually they left. After a minute or two Aunt Mary said, "Did something the MacNaughtons said offend you? You seemed even quieter than usual."

"MacNaughtons?" I repeated. I was fairly sure that was the name of the couple with the new baby, but pretending I wasn't sure gave me a few seconds to recoup.

5

"The couple who came up to our table," Uncle James explained. "He teaches at the university."

"Oh, no," I said. And then, to get them off the subject of my being quiet, "They seemed awfully old to be having a baby."

"Tut," Uncle James said. He smiled. "That could be called an ageist comment."

"Maybe," Aunt Mary put in. "But I know what Claudia means." She looked at me. "They spent years trying to get Mary pregnant, but it never worked. So they decided to adopt, only it can be a long process even after you've made up your mind, so they only got Peter a couple of months ago."

My heart started beating. "So—so he's only a couple of months old? I mean, did they get him as soon as he was born?"

"Well, the next day, or maybe the day after." She looked at me. "Why?"

"No reason," I said, struggling to sound indifferent. I felt rather than saw Aunt Mary's eyes on me. "This dish is very good," I said desperately. "What did you say it's called?"

"Pasta primavera," Uncle James said.

"I've never had it before," I babbled on.

"Considering the time you've spent in Italy," Aunt Mary commented, "that's surprising."

"I guess I've never picked it off the menu," I said. I had no idea whether I'd picked it or eaten it before or not. I just wanted to get them off the subject of the Mac-Naughtons' adopted baby.

Luckily, at that point the dessert wagon rolled by on its way to somebody else's table and distracted Uncle James.

"Wow!" he said, and pointed. "What's that rich delectable?"

"Chocolate mousse cake, sir," the waiter said in a seductive voice.

Uncle James sighed. "It's probably got a million calories."

"If not two million," Aunt Mary agreed. "But go ahead, live a little!"

To my vast relief she didn't return to the subject of the MacNaughtons' adopted baby.

When we got home I yawned, said I was tired, and went upstairs almost immediately. I wasn't tired, but I wanted to be alone.

All during my shower I thought about the MacNaughtons' baby, telling myself what a good life it would have with them. I stood under the water—first hot, then warm, then cool—for a long time, in the hope that it would help me sleep. For the past three months my sleeping had been erratic. Always before I associated poor sleeping habits with people who were at least middle-aged, such as my parents, or Uncle James and Aunt Mary. Now I knew that somebody my age could also suffer from poor sleep.

After my shower I put the newspaper I'd brought from school on the bed, propped up my pillows, got into bed and opened the paper. At home we'd always subscribed to *The New York Times* no matter where we were, and Daddy used to read it at the breakfast table, sometimes aloud, and comment on various items. So I loved going over it now. That is, I did until I hit the last page of the second section, where I saw the headline: "Adopted Child Abused."

The fear was a sickness that hit me in my deepest part and then swelled like some monster growth. Frantically I read the short news report: A six-year-old girl living in New York City with her adoptive parents had been horribly abused and died because of the abuse. Apparently the story had been reported for some time now and this was just a follow-up piece.

I searched through the paper, but there was nothing else about it. I knew now that my sleep, already sporadic, would be much worse.

That was what having a baby and having it adopted but not knowing where or with whom could do to you.

— 2 —

I was sixteen when I became pregnant.

My baby was born four months ago, just after I became seventeen. Those nine months were long, difficult, and as far as my relations with my parents went, full of turmoil. My parents, by which I mean mostly my mother—my father has always been too distant, physically and emotionally—wanted me to have an abortion. I fought that one and won. Quite why I was so determined to have the baby I'm not sure. All I knew was that I couldn't bring myself to abort the baby. I had no passionate principles on either side of the whole abortion issue. It had always been like other hotly argued political conflicts that the rest of the world marched and protested and screamed about. What counted with me was the consciousness of the soft, small living being inside me. Something that was entirely mine. When I thought of having some doctor go in and scrape it out as though it were garbage, I couldn't do it.

Both Mother and Father battled that down the line.

"Do you want the rest of your life to be ruined?" Mother asked one Saturday morning.

"I don't see why the rest of my life should be ruined. It's only nine months!"

"And just what do you intend to do those nine months? Go to the school you've been in for the past three years? I can just hear the comments now. 'Gee, Claudia, you're certainly putting on weight. Whatsa matter? Too many snacks during television?' Until, of course, it becomes obvious just where and what the weight is. You want to imagine that?" Mother hardly ever raised her voice, but her sarcasm cut like a whip.

"I've thought about that," I said. "There's a place I can go to in Vermont. It's an unwed mother's home. But they also offer school. I can finish the school year there."

"And what happens to the baby?"

"I'll put it up for adoption. That's one of the things that the school arranges."

"I see. Have you thought beyond that? When and if you marry, you're going to have to talk to your husband, whoever he is, about your having had a child, especially if, as the doctor here says, you might have a rocky time. How do you imagine he'd like that?"

"I wouldn't marry anyone without telling them."

"And you think some idealistic guy would take that in his stride."

"Come on, Liz," my father said. "This isn't the nineteen forties or even fifties. People aren't as puritanical as they used to be. You should know that. We grew up in the sixties. A lot of the old taboos were swept away!"

"And how do you think the Foreign Service would feel about you after your sixteen-year-old has a baby? Have you ever considered that?"

"If they don't like it, they can lump it. I can always get a job in a university somewhere or on a newspaper or a magazine."

I looked over at my father with surprise and gratitude. When I had my appendix out, he was in Pakistan. When my best friend got killed in an accident, he was in Finland. When I got into the depths of despair when I thought I wasn't going to get promoted to the upper school after a year when I went to not one but two different schools, he was in Argentina. In other words, whenever before I had had a crisis, he was somewhere else. Sometimes we—Mother and I—were with him for a while, whenever Mother was able to get a leave of absence from her law firm. But often we weren't. And even when we were together, his mind always seemed to be on something else. So his support of me now took me by surprise.

"Thanks for your help," Mother said bitterly, and turned back to me. "Claudia, I'm a lot older than you. "If you have an abortion now, you can forget about the whole thing. It won't be a permanent . . . well, marker in your life. Even if you can get it adopted right away, it will always be there."

"I'm going to have the baby," I said. "And if you try to force me not to, I'll run away."

"I'm just trying to point out that you don't know what you'll be letting yourself in for. If you'll just listen to—"

"No," I screamed. "NO! Stop going on and on at me!" And I ran out of the apartment.

"Claudia! Claudia! Stop!"

I could hear her voice and then my father's, calling my name. I prayed for the elevator to come and somebody

11

heard my prayer. The door opened and I got in just before they came running out of the apartment.

Luckily there were two exits to the apartment house. One was the usual one, with a doorman. The other was a back door that led into the courtyard. I left by that and was out onto the street before Mother could call the doorman.

It was December and cold. I had no coat on, and I'd run out without bag or money. I looked in the pocket of my jeans and blessed my habit of sticking loose change there. I had enough to ride a bus to a public library a few blocks away. Once I was with books, I could spend any number of hours quite happily.

Aunt Mary had said she always saw me with a crowd of other kids. What she didn't know was that I worked hard to be popular. Or, rather, Mother worked hard. She wanted me to be popular more than she wanted me to get good grades. "If you want to get on in life, then people have to like you," she said more than once.

"Being liked didn't get you into law school," Father said.

"It didn't hurt," Mother replied. "But with me—" And then she stopped. Tact wasn't her leading quality, but every now and then she was overcome with it. I knew what she wasn't saying was that she was generally accorded to be the prettiest girl in her school. By all accounts, the boys lined up ten feet deep. Father was one of many at college who scrambled to be noticed by her. And she went to law school after she was married.

"It's all right," I said. "I know I'm not as pretty as you are. Nor as popular."

"You could be if you just tried." Mother underlined the word.

So I tried hard and to a degree I succeeded. What helped even more was that Mother and Father made a big point about inviting my friends and classmates over a lot. So that was why whenever my father's brother, James, and James's wife, Mary, visited, it always seemed like I was in the middle of an admiring huddle.

I got to the library and wandered among the stacks, picking out books that looked interesting and then taking them back to one of the long tables. I read part of a book on French history, another on the Tudors and started on one of George Eliot's novels. By this time it was midafternoon, and I was ravenously hungry. I groped in my pocket to see if I had any more change. I did, but only enough to get a bus back to the apartment.

I had been all prepared for the morning sickness I'd read so much about. But I felt as fine as I ever did, and twice as hungry.

Maybe if I used the bus money for a hot dog, I'd walk back. It seemed like a good idea, so I put the books away and was going out of the library when I ran into a girl from school. She was a senior and a brain and a grind. Very uncool. She was also plain.

"Hey, what are you doing here?" she asked.

Somehow I resented her question. "What are you?"

"I'm doing some research."

She said it a little as though she'd been granted the Nobel Prize.

"That's nice."

"But what are you doing?"

I rather resented the question as though a library was the last place I'd be. "I'm also doing research."

"What on?"

"On the incidence of pregnancy in urban areas," I

made up on the spot. I was so angry with my mother that at that moment I didn't greatly care if I did give myself away.''

"Whose class is that for?"

"Miss Edwards's."

"Oh. Well, I'm going to have some lunch. What about you?"

"I'm not hungry," I said, wondering if my immortal soul would stand up under such a lie.

As soon as she disappeared I gave up the struggle and took the bus home, hoping that my parents wouldn't be there. They were, of course, and were furious when they saw me.

"We've been worried sick," Mother said. "Never do that again. If we have a—a difference, at least stay so we can talk it out!"

"If you'll stop trying to pressure me when I ask you to, then I won't run away."

There was a tense silence.

"Why aren't you at the office?" I asked, a little afraid it would bring on another explosion. "I thought you said you had stuff there that had to be finished."

"I wonder," my father said mildly.

I giggled. He folded his paper. "Will you take off again if I ask you, once more, who the father of your child is?"

It was the second big question and the one I was most afraid of.

During the past four years I'd gone to school in France, a school in Belgium, and a school in Italy. When I finally came back to school in the States—mostly because my family decided it was time I did, that is, if I wanted to be an American among Americans—I felt like an outsider,

14

not academically, but socially. As a whole, my grades were better than those in my peer group, but I wasn't much up on the boy-girl thing. The schools I'd gone to abroad had been girls' schools. We talked endlessly about boys, of course, but the customs were different. I realized when I went to an American school in the suburb in which we lived that American kids had a lot more freedom than I'd been used to. They didn't stay at school in the afternoon as long, and they didn't have as much homework. What most of them did was hang out, and I tried to hang out with them. The boys came on, but they scared me a little, and when I got scared, I dried up. I couldn't think of anything to say. What I wanted to do was split—fast, and I usually did, thinking of an excuse that didn't sound too lame.

After a while most of them decided I was a bore and a grind. The boys—or some of them—still tried to come on. Once, when I thought one of them was sort of attractive—we were in his car and he was trying to slide an arm around me—I decided to let him, but just as his hand gripped my shoulder and he started pulling me toward him, a girl came out of one of the school buildings, stopped cold, then started walking forward with a look on her face that made me want to shrivel and die.

"Ouch!" the boy, Joe, said, and removed his arm. "I thought she'd gone to ballet class."

I looked at him. "Are you—is she—?"

"Yeah," he said, stretching out his legs. "I guess you could say that."

I got out of the car, "I didn't know that you and he were—" I started as the girl came up. That was as far as

I got before she snapped, "I bet you didn't, you rotten, date-stealing little—"

"Hey, Linda," Joe said. "Don't go into orbit! It was just a joke—"

Somehow, that was the worst of all. And it proved to be the end of me as far as that school was concerned. Linda was popular and had a lot of clout. I hadn't had time to make many friends. I stayed either at the library or at home after that. Father was in Rome off and on that year, so it was mostly Mother and me.

Then her firm moved her to Washington briefly, so I went to school there. That was when she decided something had to be done about my lack of popularity, and almost every weekend she saw to it that a bunch of kids were in and out of our apartment. But in a curious way, I didn't think of them as my friends. I thought of them as Mother's, and, of course, Father's, when he was home.

Then one day in the library I met Alan. He was a lot older than I and was working on his doctorate at a local university where he also taught one or two classes. We met in the stacks among the books on French history. I asked him a question about a title and he answered with a smile. He was quiet. He didn't frighten me. In fact, he seemed almost European in his reserve, not at all like the boys I'd met who appeared to have one thing on their minds and a burning determination to achieve it in the shortest possible time so they could get on with the rest of their lives. Sort of like bagging the quarry during hunting.

We both left the library when it closed, and chatted briefly at the foot of the front steps before going home our separate ways. After that I found myself looking for him in the library, and I saw him most nights when I could get

16

there. Over the weekends Mother was involved with the parties and get-togethers that somehow seemed to coalesce at our apartment.

"Come on, do your share!" she'd sometimes say to me when she found me by myself nibbling a canape or a piece of cheese. "This party's for you."

So I'd join the nearest group and try to take part, but it never really worked. I wasn't one of them and they knew it and so did I. But Mother's eats were fabulous and famous, and of course when the gang went on to something else, I went with them because they couldn't very well not have taken me and I knew if I tried to stay, Mother would have a fit. Besides, I kept hoping that somehow something would make me feel at home, like one of them. But the girls ignored me pretty much, or at least I thought they did, and the boys tried to move from A to B so fast I'd back off.

Weeknights, Mother was content for me to be in the library, probably because I deliberately gave her the impression that I was meeting some of the gang there. The gang she thought I meant wouldn't have been caught dead in the library, but she didn't have to know that.

I saw Alan most nights when I was there, either sitting at one of the long tables, or, more often, in one of the carrels that he seemed to have a permanent fix on. Often we left together. He was shy, and I liked that. And the fact that he was older made him much more interesting than any of the boys in the gang. For one thing, we talked about something other than who was going with whom and what the latest gossip was. I once asked him a question about the French Revolution which I was studying.

He finished his answer in a coffee shop nearby, where

17

he was having a milk shake and I was having tea and a muffin. After that we went to the coffee shop a lot. I never learned much about him other than the fact that he came from Vermont and had gone to school there, because he always seemed to close down when I asked any question that seemed in the least personal. What he liked to talk about was history, economics, politics, the eighteenth century in France, the nineteenth century in England. He didn't lecture, he just talked, and since I was interested in those subjects, I loved to listen. I suppose, now, that it was because I wasn't frightened.

He was trying to remember something he'd read one night, when he suggested we go back to his room at the university where he could look it up.

I was sitting on his sofa and he was leafing through one of the many books that filled his room—on the shelves, on his desk, on the floor—when I saw a bottle behind some books on his desk.

"That's vodka," proud that I could identify it.

"That's right. Do you want some?"

I was about to refuse, when I surprised myself by saying, "Will it make me drunk?"

"Have you ever had anything alcoholic to drink?"

"Of course. Lots of times." Having lived in France, I had often had liberally watered wine at meals, but I was feeling sophisticated and wanted to seem so.

"Here." He opened a cupboard, took out two glasses, and poured some vodka in each. "Sorry about the lack of ice," he said.

"They hardly ever use ice in Europe," I said, still in my sophisticated mode.

I had never tasted vodka, or whisky or gin for that matter. My parents much preferred wine. I drank a swallow. It went down like a burning light. I coughed.

"Be careful with that," he said, laughing.

The second swallow made me feel wonderful. The shyness that had crippled me vanished. The conviction that I was plain and would never be as good-looking as my mother also vanished. I heard my own voice say, "My mother's terribly good-looking and I'm a great disappointment to her," a sentiment that had been in my mind since I had been thirteen and knew, somehow, that I wasn't going to grow much taller or prettier.

"Wherever did you get that nonsense?" Alan said, coming over and sitting on the sofa beside me. "I think you're extremely pretty."

"You do?"

"Yes," he said after a moment.

It is at that moment that my memory, on the dozens of occasions when I have tried to recall that evening, starts to blur.

"Yes," he said again. "I do." He put his hand on my face and tipped it up. Then he kissed me. It was not the first time I'd been kissed. But this wasn't a contest. It was gentle and tender. I felt it all the way down my body. I remember his hand putting his glass down on the table, then it came back and pulled me to him and then, after a while, still gently, rested on my breast.

After a while I picked up his glass—my own seemed to have vanished—and drank the rest.

"Are you sure you ought to?"

"Yes," I recall saying, and adding with great emphasis, "I do."

I remember being on the bed and looking down at his

body and my own. "I've never seen a man naked before," I said.

"Shhh!" He took my hand down to his groin. I remember a surging excitement. Then nothing. My next memory was sitting in a car in front of our apartment house.

My head was going around and around. "What time is it?"

"About twelve."

I felt wildly sick. "I'm going to throw up," I said. "Not here! Hang on, now!" He started the car and drove to a nearby park. Then he opened the door. "Be sick out there."

I stumbled out, bent double and was violently ill. He was beside me, and passed me his handkerchief when I was through.

"We'd better go back to your apartment house," he said. "What are you going to tell your family—I mean, about coming in this late?"

"I'll tell them I ran into some of the kids from school."

"How old are you?"

"Sixteen."

"Oh, God!"

I stared at him. He sounded really upset. "What's the matter?"

"You're a minor. That's what's the matter. The review panel for my appointment is coming up in a few weeks."

"What's that got to do with it?"

He pulled up beside the house. "Nothing. I devoutly hope. You'd better go in."

His voice was so different, I thought. In some way, even through my fuzziness, I felt insulted.

"I'll be all right," I said, and decided to go in. We didn't have a doorman at that hour, but I had a key. I walked in as steadily as I could. My head was whirling, but I determined not to show it. As I turned the key I looked back, but Alan had already gone. That was the last I ever saw of him.

— 3 —

Mother and Father first demanded, then pleaded, that I tell them who got me pregnant. But I never did. I knew if I told them who Alan was, they'd put pressure on him to marry me, and I was too angry and hurt for that to happen. When he kept not showing up at the library, I finally went to the university with a letter from me addressed to him and gave it in at the reception office of the main building.

"Alan Huntly," the girl behind the desk said, looking at the envelope.

"Do you know him?" I asked.

"Sure. He's a teaching fellow. But he's in France right now, doing some kind of research on his doctorate."

It was like getting kicked in the stomach. "When did he go?"

"Two or three weeks ago. Why?"

Two or three weeks meant he must have left right after I'd been in his apartment. "No reason," I said. Then, "Do you have an address for him in France?"

"I don't know. You'd have to ask the head of the history department. Who wants to know?" The girl was staring at me as though I were a bug, I thought.

22

I opened my mouth to give my name, but nothing came out.

"Anything wrong?" A man's voice said. He had come up behind the desk and was standing there.

"No," I said, hating my cowardice.

"I guess I could ask his wife," the girl said. "But she's in class right now."

It was as though something heavy had been smashed across my face. "His wife," I managed to repeat after her.

"Yes. We could leave a message for her to call you."

"No, that's okay." Somehow I got out of the building without falling down.

The next two months were a horror. I went through them in a sort of numbed state. Every now and then Mother would say, "What's the matter with you? Are you okay?"

"Fine," I always said. "Everything's great." And I'd try and act as though it were true. The get-togethers in our house went on. The gang showed up, and I tried to pretend I was having a good time. Luckily, Mother had a difficult and important legal case absorbing most of her time and attention, so she didn't ask me any awkward questions. And Father, after one or two sporadic efforts to talk to me, was sent for a while to Poland.

I tried not to think about anything when I missed my period once. It could happen to anyone, I told myself. In fact, I knew a girl who sometimes missed and didn't seem any the worse for it. Then I missed another. After that I went by myself to a well-known clinic that I knew would take tests without demanding my name or my parents' name or threaten to talk to them. After the requisite num-

23

ber of days I returned and learned that I was about ten weeks pregnant.

"It only happened once!" I said before I could stop myself.

"That's enough, even if you'd never had sex before, if it was the right time of the month and neither one of you took any precautions." She paused. "I take it you didn't."

I shook my head.

"That's very foolish." The woman looked at me in a kindly way. "Now, let me tell you your options."

That was when I found out about the school in Vermont. And even though by then I had a prejudice against Vermont because of Alan's coming from there, it seemed like the best place.

I stayed in regular school for another two months. Even though I'm short and skinny, I didn't show too much. But at the end of that time I did, and I was glad to leave my school and go up to Vermont to stay for the remaining four and a half months. The school handled the adoption, which took place two days after I had the baby. I only saw my baby for that one day. He was small and red-faced and had blue eyes and dark, curved eyelashes. Part of me longed to keep him, but the other part knew he would have a better chance with a family that could take care of him properly and give him two parents. I never saw who they were, but the school promised me that they had been fully investigated and were good people.

When I went home, home had moved to New York because my mother's law firm had transferred her again. I spent the rest of the summer there. Then Father was sent to Europe again, and this time Mother went with him. A university outside Brussels had asked her to lecture on

American law, and also offered her a year's fellowship to carry on her research for a paper she was writing on international law. "I don't like to leave you," Mother said to me. "Especially not after—" And she stopped.

"Go, please go!" I almost shouted it. The relationship between us had become badly strained since my pregnancy. I knew that I resented almost everything she said. I also knew that I shouldn't; that she had done what she had because she thought it was best for me. But it didn't make it easier.

"You know, Claudia, it's not my fault you became pregnant!"

"I know!"

"And in case you think it has, it hasn't been easy for me either."

"I'm sorry for you."

"Won't you tell me—"

"No!"

That Alan had been married all along was the wound that wouldn't heal. I knew such things happened. I just didn't think he'd be the kind of person who would do that. The hearty football adolescents that crammed our home during Mother's little get-togethers, yes. Not Alan with his quiet smile, his aloofness.

Except that he had.

I was relieved when Mother decided to go ahead with her lectures and research. I liked Aunt Mary and Uncle James. Even more, they didn't know anything about my having a baby. I made Mother promise she wouldn't tell them.

A few weeks later I read the article about the adopted child being abused and then dying.

* * *

The next morning at breakfast Aunt Mary said, as I sat down, "How did you sleep?"

"Fine," I lied. For some reason it seemed important that neither she nor Uncle James think there was anything wrong in my life.

"You don't look like you did," Uncle James said, folding his paper. It was, of course, that day's issue of the same paper I had upstairs.

"Oh? Well, I was busy studying." Which was a version of the truth. I had read and reread the paper from cover to cover to see if there were any more references to the abused child.

"Good for you! What were you studying?" Uncle James put the paper down beside him.

"Current affairs," I said. Then, "Are you going to take your paper to the college?"

"Yes. I was planning to. Why?" He looked up at me over his half glasses as he poured himself some coffee.

"Mr. O'Shea wants us to read the paper each day." I improvised.

"He teaches history, doesn't he?" Uncle James said.

"Yes."

"So is this a version of current affairs?"

"Yes."

"I think that's a good idea," Aunt Mary said. "I went to school with any number of girls who could reel off the names of the presidents but had barely heard of World War Two."

"Today they still haven't heard of World War Two, and they also haven't heard of any of the presidents," Uncle James said bitterly. He handed me the folded paper. "Here, take a look before I have to leave. If O'Shea is that eager for you to keep up with the news, then he ought to offer to buy you a subscription."

"Or Claudia can pick it up at the station newsstand."

"That's pretty far out of the way of the school," Uncle James objected.

"I don't mind," I said quickly. That's what I'd do, I thought. I'd stop by each day and pick up the paper.

"Well, you can look at the paper now for today." Uncle James said.

"After you've eaten your breakfast," Aunt Mary said. "I'd hate your parents to come back and find you'd lost weight and were looking peaked."

I swallowed my juice, skipped coffee and spooned up my cereal. Then I opened the paper.

"Not hungry?" Aunt Mary asked. "No muffin?" She was handing out a plate of muffins.

"No thanks," I said. I was glancing over the pages and turning them. *The New York Times* is not a small paper nor a short one.

"Looking for anything special?" Uncle James asked.

There was something in his voice that made me glance up. Both he and Aunt Mary were watching me.

"Not really," I said, making myself slow down.

"You seem to be more interested in local news," Uncle James said. "You skipped fast through the first section with the international news."

My heart was beating rapidly now. I knew that I had given myself away. "I just thought I'd check on the local politics, then I could look more thoroughly at the international scene when I get my own copy." I made myself hand the paper back to Uncle James. "Thanks."

He offered to drive me to the school and I accepted. I didn't want to arouse any more suspicions of any kind.

When we got there I thanked him again and strolled into the school. As soon as I saw his car drive off, I went out again and set off in the opposite direction where the station was located.

"Where are you going in such a hurry?" a voice said.

I looked quickly around. Jeff Talbot was grinning at me.

Jeff is a certified BMOC, that is, big man on campus. He's captain of the football team, is on the hockey eleven, goes out with only the most attractive girls. He's also rumored to be bright and a good student, but he reminded me of the football hearties at my previous school whom I had disliked so much. Their sole aim on a date, as far as I could make out, was to wrestle a girl into a corner of the car and then start groping her. Once I said to one of the boys who was trying to do that to me, "Why don't you try it with that girl across the street. I don't think you care who it is you're groping. Just as long as it's a female body."

"Not a bad idea," the boy said, and started opening the car door. But I got out first and ran all the way home which was, luckily, only a couple of blocks. When I told Mother about it she said, "Look, Claudia, they're only trying it on. That's part of the adolescent culture over here. You're going to have to learn how to cope with it."

"I don't feel like a person. I feel like a piece of meat," I said.

"I told your father that we'd be bringing up what amounted to a foreigner. But he wouldn't believe me. I was right. We should have stayed here." Mother had never liked living abroad that much.

Looking at Jeff brought the whole thing back. "Excuse me," I said, and pushed past him through the door.

"Hey!" he said. "What'd I do wrong? Why are you mad?"

"I'm not," I called over my shoulder. "I'm just in a hurry!"

It was downhill to the station, so I ran there without too much trouble. I not only bought *The New York Times*, but also the *Daily News* and two other metropolitan papers.

"Want a bag?" the newsman asked.

I was about to refuse, when I thought, if they were in a bag I might avoid comment. "Thanks."

"Sorry, I gave away my last," the newsman said after a moment. "Shoulda kept my mouth shut."

"It's okay."

Going back uphill wasn't quite as easy. I not only had the papers, I also had my books. The papers weren't heavy, but they were bulky and kept sliding, so I stood on a corner between lights, trying to juggle them.

"Want a lift?" It was Mr. O'Shea.

I was about to refuse when I decided I could use one. "Thanks," I said, and got into the car beside him. Lamely I added, "I didn't realize papers were that bulky."

"You really took my instructions about keeping up with the news to heart, didn't you? What did you think of yesterday's *Times*?"

My mind was completely blank, except, of course, for the item about the abused child. As the silence stretched out I panicked. "I thought the piece about Congress was fascinating," I said, praying there had been such a piece. I had a feeling I'd seen a headline mentioning the word *Congress*.

And then my heart jumped again when he said, "Which one? The one in the first section about the Boland Amendment, or the one on the congressional leadership in the second part?''

I had no idea, but at the moment we drew up outside school. "I'm awfully sorry, Mr. O'Shea, but I'm going to be late for my first class. Thanks a lot for the lift.''

He smiled, leaned across me and pushed the door open. "Don't think you can get out of the question, though. I'll ask you that later.''

By later I'd have had a chance to know what he was talking about, I thought, sick with relief, as I tore into the school. I didn't have a class then, so I went straight to the library where I could look at the papers.

There was nothing in the *Times* about the abused child, but there was in one of the other papers I picked up, plus an article on child abuse, and an editorial saying it was becoming an epidemic. "Be careful to whom you give your baby to be put up for adoption,'' the editorial said. "And, if you want to adopt, be careful from whom you get your baby. There's money in these negotiations, and many unscrupulous people take advantage of desperate mothers and equally desperate families. . . .''

But the school in Vermont had been recommended by the clinic I had gone to. It must be all right, I told myself. Then I read the article.

At least the abused child in New York had been a girl and had been much older than my baby would be now. But baby boys, the same age as mine, had been rescued from homes where they had been adopted and locked in closets, or were covered with bruises, or were burned. Or they had not been rescued in time and it was their bodies that told of their abuse.

I sat there, staring at the article. My heart was beating rapidly and I felt sick.

"Are you all right, Claudia?" When I looked up I realized that the librarian who was standing beside me must have asked the question more than once. Everyone at the table was looking at me.

"Yes," I managed to say. "Yes, I'm all right."

"You're white as a sheet," the girl sitting opposite me said. I knew her slightly because her locker was near mine. "Are you sure you're okay?"

"Yes. I—I ate something last night that upset me. I think it was just a—a tummy upset."

"I'm going to call the nurse's office now," the librarian said. "I think you should go up there."

To my almost sick relief, the bell rang out.

"I'll go after I've been in class," I said, frantically collecting my things.

"Here, don't you want your papers?" And a boy who had been setting next to me picked them up off the floor where they had fallen.

"Oh, thanks!" And I scuttled out of there as fast as I could.

I was seriously thinking of cutting class altogether, when I saw the librarian come out of the library. To leave the school building by the least noticeable route would take me straight past her, so I went in the opposite direction, aiming for the front door. But just as I approached, I saw the principal go in, and I knew that he would see me as I went by. Ours is not a big school. Kids don't go in and out much during the day. I was certain he would wonder why I was leaving and would probably make inquiries as to why I wasn't going instead to Miss Strickland's class, where I was due for this hour. I stopped and paused. Then I looked behind me. The librarian was coming up fast. In

31

the classroom to my left Miss Strickland, senior English teacher, was just sitting down.

I went in and chose a desk as far back as I could and hoped Miss Strickland wouldn't notice me. Everybody was afraid of Miss Strickland. The rumor was she was past sixty and near retirement age. But she didn't show any signs of retirement or being too old to teach. In fact, she was the toughest teacher in school. It was harder to get a good grade from her than anyone else. I'd have been over-joyed to have cut that particular class, but caught between the librarian and the principal's office, I decided to postpone my departure.

I put my book satchel down on the floor, opened the book of English poetry that we were currently studying, and started thinking about what I now knew was the most important project of my life: How I could find out where my baby was and with whom, and whether it was safe and well looked after.

— 4 —

But I didn't get much chance to plot what I was going to do.

"Claudia Ransom," Miss Strickland said. "Tell us what you thought of Keats's 'Ode to Melancholy'." I must have looked blank, because she added dryly, "Your assignment from Wednesday."

It had gone out of my head, of course. I couldn't now even remember her assigning it.

I felt almost as though she had asked me a question in a language I'd never heard before.

"You think it's gorgeous," a quiet voice mumbled just behind me. It was a boy, but other than that I didn't know who he was.

"I—it's beautiful," I said.

"It's reassuring to hear you say so. In this day of no rhyme and no meter and, as far as one can see, often no structure or content, it's nice to hear a young student praise one of the older forms."

By the time she'd finished saying that I had remembered that 1) she liked pre-twentieth-century verse, 2) she'd written a book on Keats that had, so the rumor told, had good reviews, and 3) she knew perfectly well I hadn't read it.

"I didn't get to read it," I said.

"Well, at least you're honest—even if belatedly. I thought we were going to be treated to second-hand Jeff Talbot for a while."

So it was Jeff. I was glad I had, in effect, turned down his offer after the first attempt.

"Please speak to me after class," she went on. "Meg Fullerton, did you manage to read the ode?"

Meg had read the ode. She didn't actually look across the room at me as she discussed Keats and his rhyming system and metaphors, but I felt she did. I had managed to get two A's on my essays when she had been given one A- and one B+, both from Miss Strickland. No one else had come higher than a C+.

After class I walked up to Miss Strickland's desk. Any hope I might have had that she would have forgotten she said she wanted to speak to me vanished when she looked up at me.

"It's not like you not to have done the assignment," she said abruptly. "What happened to you?"

"Nothing," I said, lying as boldly as I could.

She stared at me for a moment. Then she said, "I don't believe you, but it's your affair. You started off very well. If you have college plans, especially if they include good schools, then you're going to have to keep up your work." She paused. "I'm aware that there are a lot of distractions when you're seventeen, but I don't think they're important enough to threaten your future. One thing puzzles me, though. You're very bright. I'm sure you know that, so I'm not giving you undue praise. But I'm surprised you're older than most of the other students." She paused. "Did you lose a year for any reason?"

Curiously, the school hadn't asked that when Uncle

James applied for entry for me, or if it had, he must have made up some reason. I had the grades, of course, from the school in Vermont, but there was still a lot of lost time. And I was older than most of the juniors, though not the oldest.

"If you don't want to answer, I certainly can't make you."

Miss Strickland was not like any other teacher I had ever had. For one thing she was older. For another, she was tougher.

She picked up her books. "Well, do your homework in future. You can do well, if you want to and try hard, but not if you don't. To make up for not having read the ode, you can write me a short piece—two pages—on it. Have it done by the next class." She glanced at me. For a moment I thought I saw a glimmer of humor. "As well, of course, as doing your homework."

As soon as I could I went back to the library to see if there were any pieces in the newspapers about abused children that I'd missed.

But there weren't, and any specific babies that were mentioned were either the wrong age or the wrong sex or both. If I could just find who had adopted my own baby and make sure that he was all right and the people were good parents, then I could forget the whole thing and go on with my life. But until I did find out I knew I couldn't think about anything else.

I was about to throw the papers in the library wastebasket when I thought it might be safer to take them out and put them in a public litter basket. It was all very well to say that Mr. O'Shea wanted us to keep up with current affairs, but no other student was buying every newspaper she could lay a hand on.

It was terribly important that no one knew what I was looking for.

I stuffed the papers in my bag and left the library. In the hall I hesitated. My next class was Mr. O'Shea's, but I had a free period before then. I decided to go to a public phone and call the school up in Vermont. There was a teacher there I liked, a Miss Halsey. She taught writing and didn't treat the girls at the school like fallen women, the way some of the teachers did. If I explained to her why I wanted to know who adopted my baby, she might be able to get the information for me. Because, of course, it was against the rules for any girl to try to find out who adopted her child. That was part of the agreement a pregnant girl had to sign before she entered the school—she was not to try to discover who had her child or where it was.

But I couldn't worry about that now. My baby's safety came first.

I was about to walk out of the school building when Jeff Talbot suddenly appeared again. "Hello again!"

"Are you following me?"

"Why would I do that?"

"Because it's all too much of a coincidence. I bumped into you before and now here."

"And to think I tried to help you in class with old Strickland!"

"You didn't want to help me. You just wanted me to look like a fool."

He put his hand out, past my shoulder, and leaned against the wall, "Say not so, fair one. And anyway, where are you off to in such a hurry?"

I shouldn't have done it. Jeff was not somebody to alienate. But I was suddenly so angry at him that I pushed my hand against the inside of his elbow as he leaned his arm against the wall. It took him by surprise. His arm doubled up, pushing his face against the wall.

"Hey!" he said, rubbing his nose. "Watch what—"

But by that time I was down the steps and running towards the town mall where I knew there were plenty of phones. This was where having a car would have been useful, but I hadn't realized how much I might need one, and after everything that had happened, I didn't think my parents would be willing to get me one.

The mall proved farther away than I had realized, but I finally came to a phone on a corner and put down my books while I groped for change.

"How much does a call to Vermont cost?" I asked the operator.

It came to a dollar fifty, and I knew I didn't have all that much in change. I'd have to go into a store and get some change.

But getting a store to hand over a lot of change was not as easy as I thought. Checkout places were not that fond of giving change. Finally I went into a bookstore and found a sympathetic clerk who gave me eight quarters for two dollars, and dimes and nickels for a third.

I thought I'd never forget the phone number of the school, which I had hated, but I found I couldn't get quite the right order of numbers, so I called information, was given the correct number and punched it out.

But when I asked for Miss Halsey a rather breathless voice on the other end said she'd left.

"Left for the day?" I asked, glancing at my watch. It was not yet lunch, and our classes there had been long.

"No, left the school," the voice said.

I couldn't believe it. I knew she'd been there for at least ten years.

"But she can't have!"

" 'Fraid she has. Want to talk to anyone else?"

"What happened?"

"Don't know. I've only been here a couple of weeks, but the rumor is that there was a dustup and she was out of here in less than a week."

"A dustup? What about?"

"Who knows. Maybe a bad report on one of the adoptees. Can I help you with anything else?"

"What bad report?" In my anxiety I almost shrieked it.

I heard then a murmur of voices. There was a sound, and then another voice—a much older voice which I immediately recognized—said, "Who is this?"

It was Miss Gaitskill, the school principal. I'd never liked her and she never liked me. I wasn't entirely sure why, except that we seemed to get off on the wrong foot on the first day I was there.

I hung up quickly. I knew that I wouldn't be able to get any information from Miss Gaitskill about who adopted my baby.

I was standing there in the phone booth, wondering who in the school I could call next, when there was a hammering on the glass door behind me. I turned around. An angry-looking man was standing there. He pushed the door partly open, jamming it into me. "If you're not going to use the phone, let somebody else use it!"

Reluctantly, I picked up my books and left the booth.

"Thanks," he said sarcastically.

"You're welcome," I said with equal sarcasm.

If I was not to miss Mr. O'Shea's class I had to get back. By this time I had read the two pieces about Congress, so I was prepared to answer his question if he kept me afterward, but he didn't, which was just as well, because I spent the time in class trying to remember the names of the other teachers I thought might help me, or any of the other girls who were there when I was.

No teachers came to mind, at least none like Miss Halsey, who, even if she wasn't able to help me, wouldn't have told Miss Gaitskill or the other teachers what I was after. But I did recall the names of two girls, one of whom left at about the time I did, but the other arrived only just before I left. Her name was Trudy Shannon and she was only fifteen. Suddenly in my mind I could see her—tall, rather heavy, red-haired, not very attractive, and frightened. Under the freckles her face was white and set. Her expression never seemed to change. For meals we all sat at tables that seated ten, with teachers or caretakers at either end and four girls on each side. I was never quite sure how they picked which new girl would sit at what table, but once the selection was made, it never changed. Trudy sat opposite me, and I often watched her putting small bites of food in her mouth and only speaking when she was spoken to.

For some reason I took a liking to her. Maybe because she reminded me of myself, although since she was tall and red-haired and heavy and I am small and dark and skinny, I'm not quite sure why I felt that. Perhaps it was because in a school where almost every girl was an outsider in that she had landed up pregnant without intending to be so, and had made the decision to have the baby, Trudy seemed more of an outsider than anyone else. In the brief time we were there together she never seemed to laugh or talk or joke with anybody.

One day when the girl who sat beside her wasn't at lunch—probably she wasn't feeling well—I switched places so that I could talk to her.

If it had been any other teacher but Miss Halsey, I would have been asked why I changed and sent back to my original place—the school was run on very old-fashioned disciplinary lines. Miss Halsey saw the change but made no comment.

"Hi," I said when we sat down. "Where do you come from?" I knew her name because she had been introduced at the first meal she had attended.

"Boston."

"I'm from New York. How far along are you? You don't show at all."

"I don't show because I was already fat. About five months."

"Do you know what it's going to be?"

"No."

"Don't you want to know?"

"I don't care."

I heard it then, the anger in her voice, and decided not to pursue the subject, at least not at the table.

That night in the free time right after dinner I walked over to her in the living room. "You sounded angry at lunch today. Are you angry about being pregnant?"

She looked up at me. "Yes. Aren't you?"

I was very angry at Alan, but I wasn't consciously angry at being pregnant—at least I hadn't thought of it that way to myself. I suppose I'd been too busy being determined not to let Mother force me to have an abortion. "I don't think so—I'm not sure."

40

"Then you must have wanted to get pregnant."

"No—at least, I don't think I thought about it that way. It—the sex part—only happened once."

She made a funny sound. "You're lucky!" Then she looked at me. "I guess he wasn't a member of your family."

"Why—what do you mean?"

"I don't want to talk about it."

"But—"

"No," she said, and got up. "I'm going to the movie."

They showed movies in the big living room every night, mostly old-fashioned movies without graphic sex or violence—lots of movies from the fifties. I found them boring, so I didn't go much. I usually stayed in the living room and read. But most of the girls did go, even though they made fun of the movies afterward.

I shrugged and stayed in the living room with my book that night. I was determined to go to as good a college as I could and major in English and art because I wanted to be a writer, maybe a writer of children's books, which I'd also illustrate. But that was a secret wish that I hadn't confided to anyone. I knew I'd lose a year, so I found out what books most of the colleges taught, and was reading my way through them. The one I was reading now was *Tess of the D'Urbervilles*. One of the teachers asked what it was about. If you were sixteen or under, Miss Gaitskill was strict about what you read, because she didn't think girls who were already in trouble should read what she called immoral books.

"It's about a poor girl who tries to help her family," I said, knowing that she approved of poor people who tried to improve their lot.

"Oh, well that's all right," she said.

Miss Halsey had been on duty when Miss Gaitskill, who had come suddenly into the living room, asked that. When the principal had gone, Miss Halsey said dryly, "You censored that pretty heavily, didn't you?"

"What do you think would have happened if I'd said it's about a girl who had an illegitimate baby and at the end killed the father?"

"Yes," Miss Halsey said. "I see what you mean." She hesitated. "Are you enjoying it?"

"It's sad, but I like it."

"You plan to go to college?"

"Yes."

"Good. You do that."

She wasn't like most of the other teachers. I was sure she wouldn't tell on me if she saw me do something I wasn't supposed to.

Thinking about her now, as Mr. O'Shea went on about the problems in China, I realized that even though she was a lot younger, she reminded me of Miss Strickland.

"Claudia!" I came to and saw that once again I'd been mentally off somewhere and that probably Mr. O'Shea had been calling my name several times.

"Sorry," I said quickly. "Yes?"

"How do you think the European nations should react to the uprising in China, given their own recent history?"

I had only the foggiest notion of what had happened in China, and none at all of what had been said in class. But I knew I had to make something up.

"I think they should act the way their people—peoples want them to react."

"And what is that?"

"Well, opinions are divided."

42

"In fact," Mr. O'Shea said, "you don't know what I'm referring to, do you?"

There was a silence. "No," I said.

I knew he would want to see me after the class, so as soon as the bell rang I ran out of there while two or three of the other kids were crowded around his desk asking him questions. Then I headed toward the cafeteria. In my head I could hear my mother's voice: "A little more of this kind of behavior, Claudia, and you won't graduate."

The thought of that made me feel sick.

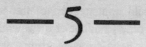

I spent the rest of the afternoon in school trying hard to concentrate in class, but I wasn't too successful. My mind kept going back to making some plan of action. Finally I gave in and wrote in my notebook:

Plan:
1) Try to find Miss Halsey and/or Trudy Shannon.

Even if I found Trudy, I wasn't sure how she could help me dig out from the school the names of the people who adopted my baby, but I was certain Miss Halsey could.

The trouble was, there was no 2) because if I couldn't find Miss Halsey or Trudy, then I didn't know what to do.

Luckily, I didn't get called on in the two afternoon classes. As soon as they were over I went to the phone booth in the mall. But somebody else had got there first. He was a boy about my age, and from his T-shirt which said MILTON'S ICE CREAM—THE BEST IN TOWN on the front and back, I knew he was one of those who worked in the ice cream parlor next to the supermarket. This cheered me, because I thought it meant he had to get back to his job. But I was wrong, it meant he was on his break or lunch hour or just goofing off. After standing outside for a while and watching, I realized he must have got somebody to call him back on the phone in the booth, because he was leaning against one wall of the booth talking as though he had the rest of the day (which maybe he had) and in the minutes I'd been there, hadn't put in any money.

After what seemed like a long time I walked around to where he was facing. He simply turned and faced the opposite way. I banged on the door. He curved his hand around the mouthpiece of the receiver so the noise wouldn't interfere.

I was furious. Angrily, I rattled the door once more, making as much noise as I could.

The door flew open, the boy looked out, and said, "Get lost!"

"That's a public phone. Other people need to use it!"

"So find another one!" And he slammed the door shut.

"I wouldn't bother with that phone," a voice said from behind me. "I think he's in for the duration."

I turned. It was Miss Strickland. She was looking down at me from her considerable height. There, with the sun on her face, I realized her eyes were a clear blue and that at one time she must have been quite beautiful. Tendrils of her wavy gray-dark hair were blowing around her face. She pushed them away. "If it's an important call you can come to my apartment to make it. I live just the other side of the mall."

I was sorely tempted, but the calls I had to make were long distance, and I wasn't sure I could keep the reason for them confidential.

"Thanks, but I have to go now anyway."

She smiled, raised her hand and walked on.

* * *

That night in bed I spent a long time trying to figure out how I could find Miss Halsey. I knew her first name, Prunella, which was considered weird by the kids in the school (who called her The Prune) but would make her relatively easy to look up in a directory. But I had no idea where her home was. Then, just before I drifted off to sleep, an idea occurred to me.

I could call the school in Vermont again, this time pretending to be a teacher from the school I was at now, requesting the Vermont school to transmit my credits. Of course they'd done it once before when I started at the school, but I could say they'd been lost. And then I could pretend I had to question Miss Halsey about something.

As though released by that, I went to sleep immediately, but I had a horrible dream of children crying. In my dream, when I went to investigate why they were crying, a little boy showed me his bruised arms and said, "It's your fault—"

I woke up suddenly, my heart pounding. I knew then I'd never be able to sleep or relax until I found out who had my son.

The next day I collected some quarters from my piggy bank and, during lunch, went to the phone booth outside the mall.

It was busy again. I waited. And waited.

Then I decided to go and look for another one. I finally found one at the other end of the mall. It, too, was busy. But the woman who was in it finally hung up and left.

I called information in the Boston area for Gertrude Shannon or Trudy Shannon or T. Shannon and drew a blank. That is, I got the numbers of three T. Shannons, but two of them didn't answer and the third was a man who said he'd never heard of a Trudy Shannon.

So I called the school in Vermont, put on my oldest voice, and said I was calling from the school Claudia Ransom now attended and would like to check something on her transcript.

"Just a minute, please," the girl said.

I prayed she wouldn't put me through to Miss Gaitskill and was relieved to hear a voice I didn't recognize answer. I went through my speech again.

"I see, which course did you want to query?"

"It was, I believe, a course taught by a Miss Halsey. Maybe I could speak to her."

"I'm sorry, she isn't here anymore. I'll see if I can get Miss—"

I broke in quickly. "Maybe I could call her at her home or new job and talk to her."

"Just a minute."

I was standing there, feeling pleased with myself and praying that she would come back with the information I wanted when I heard Miss Gaitkill's voice again. "Hello? This is Miss Gaitskill. What is it you wanted to know?"

I panicked and hung up.

A minute later, of course, I realized the mess I could have landed myself in. All the operator or the second person I talked to had to do was to tell Miss Gaitskill that it was Claudia Ransom's school calling, and she could phone the school. I could feel my heart start pounding and then skipping. My palms felt suddenly wet.

There was a banging on the door. I looked outside. Three people were lined up and the first one jerked open the door. "If you're finished you oughta let somebody else use the phone."

I wasn't finished. But I was too muddled and scared to know what to do next.

I left and went into the mall courtyard and sat on the stone wall surrounding a small fountain.

"You look as though the whole world has deserted you," a voice said. I looked up. Jeff Talbot was there, a plastic bag in his hand with the name of the mall sports shop on it.

"Sometimes I feel that way," I said before I had a chance to think clearly.

"I haven't," he said, and sat down on the wall beside me. Then he reached out and put his hand on my leg.

I don't know what happened to me then. Suddenly Alan Huntly, who had made me pregnant and then left me, plus my parents, who tried to force me to have an abortion, plus all the people I couldn't trust seemed to loom up over me. And now this football oaf was trying to make me in public. I got up to walk away.

"Hey! Don't go. Let me show you how undeserted you are!" And he reached out with his hand.

It was so easy. He was sitting on the wall, leaning back, laughing. I gave a shove and he fell into the fountain. It was only about a foot deep, so he lay there for a moment looking utterly astonished.

"What the—"

I took off. I ran as fast as I could out of the mall and in the opposite direction from the school and finally landed in front of a big apartment complex, out of breath.

It took me a moment to realize it was the place where Miss Strickland lived. I stood at the edge of the drive, staring. By this time Miss Gaitskill would have called the school and everybody there would know about my baby. How could I have been so stupid when I thought I was so brilliant? And Jeff Talbot, dripping wet, would be out for my blood.

There was another low wall, this time around a sort of flower and shrub garden. I glanced at my watch and sat down at it. My next class started in ten minutes. But I somehow didn't think it made any difference. No matter what happened, I was in trouble.

I stared at the flowers and thought about the flowers on the grounds of the school in France. I had liked that school, at least I had after my French became good enough for me to talk to people. The same with the school in Italy. I'd never been at school anywhere where I stayed long enough to be part of a group, have long-term friends I could count on. Always, always, always I felt I had to be extra nice just to have people put up with me. Except, of course, with the boys in the town I was in before I met Alan, with their groping hands and their indifference to anything except scoring . . .

And then I thought about Alan, who was so different— I thought, and I remembered Trudy's question: "Are you angry about being pregnant?" How could I have said no?

If I hadn't got pregnant I wouldn't be in the mess I was in now, and my baby wouldn't be in danger of being abused and mistreated . . . all the stories I had read, all I'd heard on television news, echoed in my head. "He was beaten around the head, he was tied to the chair, his body had bruises and burns—"

"Claudia, what's the matter? Why are you crying?"

Miss Strickland was standing in front of me. I looked up at her and saw an expression of great kindness on her face. It was more than I could bear and I heard myself start to sob.

"Come along," she said. "The door's just over there. We can go in the back entrance.

Afterward, when I tried to remember every moment of that time, I had a vague impression of a single elevator, and Miss Strickland's voice saying, "This is a service elevator, but there's no reason we can't use it." Then we were in a hallway and she was opening her door. A bark sounded from inside. "That's Boswell, thinking he's warning away robbers. She opened the door and a beautiful golden retriever flung himself at her. "Come in," she said.

When I had time to notice, I saw I was in a big, airy room with high ceilings and a view of the foothills that seemed to go on for miles. But at that moment all I was aware of was Miss Strickland's hand on my shoulder. "Come over here and sit down," she said. And when we were sitting on a sofa, "Can you tell me what's distressing you?"

So I blundered out with the whole story, about Alan and getting pregnant and the school in Vermont and my baby being adopted and the awful things I had read that had happened to adopted children and my efforts to find out who had my baby and whether he was all right.

"I see," she said when I'd finished. "That's quite a burden you're carrying, isn't it?" She hesitated. "I take it you haven't told your uncle and aunt."

"No. I don't want them to know."

"I understand. But your uncle might be able to help you. Inquiries by him would probably get further than those by you."

Curiously, I hadn't thought about that. And what she said was probably true. "You might be right, Miss Strickland, but I don't want to tell them. There must be a way

I can find out for myself." I fished for a tissue and wiped my tears and nose.

Miss Strickland got up. "You think the school in Vermont will call the school here this afternoon and, in trying to find out who called, reveal the whole business?"

"Yes. That Miss Gaitskill, the principal in Vermont, was absolutely"—I searched around for the right word. "Absolutely relentless. She always made a girl feel—" I stopped.

"Feel what?" Miss Strickland had gone over to a table on which there was a phone and was looking for something. But she turned around when she asked that.

"Guilty. Bad. Fallen. Anything that happened to us we deserved. That kind of thing. I'm sure she'd be delighted to tell the school here—Miss Bruce, the principal, and the others—what kind of school it was and why I was there."

"The you-must-reap-what-you-sow way of looking at things."

"What do you mean?" I hadn't meant to ask it so sharply, but that phrase, 'reaping what you sow' seemed to come up a lot when I was at school there.

Miss Strickland had been looking in a directory, but she glanced up now over the glasses she'd put on.

"It's just a quote from the Bible. But it's an essential part of the puritan ethic."

"What quote?"

She smiled. " 'Be not deceived, God is not mocked, for whatsoever a man soweth that shall he also reap.' "

I knew I'd heard it before somewhere—almost certainly at the school—and I could feel every hackle I had stand up.

"That's a pretty grim way of looking at things. And it's

not true. What about all the people who cheat and steal and never get caught."

"How do you know they don't get caught and have to pay in some way, sometime?"

"I read in some paper or other that for every man who is caught embezzling on Wall Street there're six who do the same thing and get away with it."

"But that quote doesn't say in what way people pay."

"What do you mean?"

She smiled. "I can't balance the books for every human being who has ever sinned. That's not exactly my job. But I did know of one case that sort of illustrates what I meant. There was a man known to my family. He was a sharp trader in the financial world. Anybody who ever worked with him knew it. The government never caught him. But one day one of his sons, who had never known this about his father and had always rather idealized him, discovered it. He was so horrified, he confronted his father. His father more or less admitted it with a 'so what?' attitude. The son left home that day and the father never saw him again, because his son committed suicide in a drug overdose a year later. Don't you think there's enough cause and effect there to make it a punishment?"

"And you're saying I should be punished?"

"Whoa—don't leap to conclusions like that! I was simply answering your question as to whether the quote was true or not."

"I'm sorry," I said after a minute. "I didn't mean to jump down your throat that way. Especially—especially after you'd been so kind."

Miss Strickland was dialing. "Jean," she said after a minute. "I've been expecting a call from a school in Vermont this afternoon. I was wondering if it had come through. It has? Did anyone take it? Fine. Let me have the name and number."

"I was standing now, facing her. "Who called?" I asked.

"Miss Gaitskill. Your crime-and-punishment lady." Miss Strickland looked at me. "You were in luck. That is, our own headmistress is away at a conference. I can call your Miss Gaitskill back. Jean gave me the number. Now, what do you want me to say?"

"What I want is to find Miss Halsey. She's the only one who might find out where my baby is. Her or Trudy Shannon."

"She or Trudy Shannon," Miss Strickland murmured. "The grammarian in me dies hard."

"She or Trudy Shannon, then," I said.

"Do you think there's any chance, if I told Miss Gaitskill about your anxiety and worry after all the stories you read, that she'd give me any information herself about where and with whom she placed your baby?"

"No, and if she thought that was what you were trying to get at, she'd—I don't know what she'd do—but she'd do anything to stop you. She thinks that our not knowing is part of the punishment for immoral behavior."

"Is that what she really thinks, or are you projecting this on her?"

"What do you mean?"

Miss Strickland hesitated. "It's a very common dynamic in people. If on some level you think you're guilty of something, but your conscious mind or self denies it, it will then seem to you that all kinds of people are pointing the finger of guilt at you. That is, you project your own repressed sense of guilt, the sense of guilt you don't admit to yourself you have, onto somebody else. And that person becomes to you the accuser, whether or not he or she is."

"That's stupid," I said angrily.

Miss Strickland's eyes looked at me over her glasses. "All right," she said. "Would you like me to call Miss Gaitskill and see if I can get any information out of her? I don't guarantee I can, but I'm willing to try."

By this time I was angry at Miss Strickland, but I decided I needed her help, so I swallowed the anger. "Yes. Please."

I watched her dial the number.

"Miss Gaitskill please," she said. Then she waited. "Miss Gaitskill? I am returning the call you made to the St. Albans School in Bainbridge." There was a pause. "No, I'm not the principal. Miss Bruce is away at a conference." There was a long silence while Miss Strickland listened. Then she said, "I think there was a question about the transcript, but I believe she wanted to talk to a Miss Halsey who taught Claudia Ransom English." Another pause. "And you don't know where she is? What a pity! Well, since I think there was a question of the clarity of the transcript regarding Claudia's English grade, perhaps you'd just send a copy of that. Thank you. Oh—no, Claudia's doing very well." And she hung up.

"You didn't find out where Miss Halsey is."

"I'm afraid not. Apparently she simply took off without leaving any forwarding address behind her, and the old address they had for her isn't valid anymore."

I sat down again on the sofa. Frustration and misery seemed to come back in waves. There was a silence.

Miss Strickland got up. "If it's any consolation, I see what you mean about Miss Gaitskill. There is, indeed, a Javert-like quality about her."

"What do you mean, Javert?"

"Javert was the policeman in Victor Hugo's great novel, *Les Misérables*, who pursued the hero, Jean Valjean, to the bitter end.

"What happened?"

"Why don't you read it and find out? Here, you can borrow this." And she handed me a thick book.

"Thanks," I said.

"Try it. In the meantime, I'll see if I can come up with any brilliant ideas as to how to find your child."

I looked at her. She was smiling. "I didn't mean to be rude," I said. "It's just that—I don't see why I should be punished. It's Alan who should be. He's the one who deceived me."

"By not telling you he was married?"

"Yes."

"I wonder where his wife was while he was—er—entertaining you in his room."

Curiously, I hadn't even thought of that. "I don't know. Maybe she was away. I wonder how she'd feel if she knew."

"You mean, you're thinking of telling her?" Miss Strickland was looking at me. "Or threatening Alan with telling her?"

"Why should he get off scot-free?"

"But I thought the idea was to make sure your baby's all right. Not to deliver punishment yourself."

I got up slowly. "Yes," I said. "I guess you're right. Thanks for your help."

I was about to leave when she came over and put her hand briefly on my shoulder. "What happened to you happens to thousands of girls. I understand you need to find out how your baby is. But try not to change it into punishing Alan.''

"Why shouldn't he be punished? It was all his fault!''

"You mean you were unconscious when it was conceived? He raped you?''

I shrugged her hand off. "No, I wasn't raped. And I wasn't unconscious. But I was . . . well, he'd given me something to drink and I wasn't used to it.''

"And he forced it down your throat?''

"You're as bad as Miss Gaitskill! You want to punish me too!''

"No, I don't want to punish you. I agree that he should have told you he was married, that he probably shouldn't have given you anything to drink—certainly not since you were underage. But you weren't a completely passive player in this drama, were you?''

Something I'd been fighting off was threatening to overwhelm me. I stepped back. "Thanks a lot for your help.'' Then I was through the door and down the hall to the elevator. I waited for it, so angry I was shaking. She was right about one thing: It was a heavy burden and I knew now I had to carry it alone.

— 6 —

I bought all the newspapers at the newsstand on the way home and then went up to my room to read them.

The story about the little boy who had been found tied up in an apartment, filthy and hungry, had disappeared from the big metropolitan daily, but the three tabloids devoted columns to his condition, to the foster care he was now in, to quotations from psychiatrists and child therapists as to what lasting damage such an experience could do to a child so young.

Of course, he was older than my baby, who would now be only four and a half months. But while I knew it couldn't be he, I also knew what terrible harm placing him with the wrong people could do.

I then read about a six-month-old girl who had been flung out of a window, about three foster children who had been left alone in a house to which they had set fire, and a detailed study of some of the babies and children brought into the emergency rooms of hospitals around the country.

I was just finishing when there was a knock on my door.

"Dinner," Aunt Mary called. "Are you all right? I didn't see you when you came home."

"I'm fine." I said with all the breezy conviction I could

put in my voice. In the meantime I was frantically stuffing the papers into the bottom drawer of the bureau. "I'll be down in a minute."

While I closed the drawer and combed my hair I came to a decision. I was going to go to Boston to see if I could find Trudy Shannon. I couldn't spend more endless hours trying to use a phone booth that always seemed occupied by somebody else. And the way I felt now, just phoning wasn't urgent or immediate enough.

What I wanted to do was take off that minute, but common sense told me that if I did, I'd be tracked down in nothing flat. I had to give myself some lead time before Uncle James and Aunt Mary were aware that I had gone, and before the school thought to tell them.

You must get into a good college. Mother's words rang through my mind. Taking off now and cutting school would hardly be the best way of achieving that. Well, it was too bad, but first things came first. And my baby's health and welfare came before anything else. Whatever doubts I might have had about that originally, they were now gone.

All through dinner, while I answered polite questions and chatted away as though nothing had happened, I planned how and when I would go.

Only once did anyone say anything that indicated I wasn't as together as the fine act I was putting on would indicate.

"Are you okay?" Uncle James said abruptly, right after dinner, as I was helping to clear up.

"Yes, of course," I said, wondering if the hammering of my heart could possibly be heard. I cleared my throat. "Why?"

He didn't say anything for a moment. Then, "I'm not sure. I—er—just wondered."

"Your uncle is inclined to be overimaginative," Aunt Mary said indulgently.

"Anybody want to take in a movie?" Uncle James said.

It was the last thing I wanted to do. I wanted to stay home and plan. But I thought if I said I'd like to go to a movie I'd allay any suspicion going around.

"Terrific," I said. "I'll just go up and get my bag."

But while I was up there the phone rang. I heard Aunt Mary answer it and stood, frozen, while I strained to hear what she was saying. When it turned out to be a friend of hers from some charity they're both involved in, I felt sick with relief. In a moment there was a knock on my door. "Claudia?"

"Come in," I said, looking around to make sure there was no telltale newsprint showing anywhere.

Aunt Mary opened the door. "I'm afraid the movie idea has to be postponed. That was Gloria down at the church. She and I are supposed to be managing this festival and sale tomorrow, and the custodian hasn't shown. Which means we have to clean the place before anything can be put up. I'm sorry!"

"That's absolutely all right," I said, delighted, and then frightened that I sounded too pleased. "I'm disappointed, of course. But I guess we can do it another time."

"That's what I told James." She hesitated. "Sometimes his funny intuitions are on target. You *are* okay, aren't you? I mean, there's nothing wrong."

"Nothing." I said, looking her straight in the eye. I don't much like to lie, but my baby came first.

"All right. I'm afraid I'm going to be late tonight, so I may not see you until tomorrow morning."

"Good night, Aunt Mary," I said, kissing her and feeling like Judas as I did.

* * *

It was too good a chance not to take. I had been half planning to postpone my departure until tomorrow morning when I would go in the usual way to school, but instead I'd bike to the bus terminal. I'd have to leave my bike there and would probably never see it again, but that couldn't be helped.

Now, if I could wait until Uncle James looked settled in for the night, I could slip out the back door, get my bike, and go to the terminal. Aunt Mary was not expecting to see me until tomorrow morning. And despite his unnerving question at dinner, Uncle James had never shown the faintest signs of wanting to have a private conversation with me. There was no reason he would tonight. But what about their worry and concern if I just took off? They'd been nothing but kind. Then I thought about my baby again and again told myself that first things came first.

The one thing that made me feel bad about all this was Samantha. Uncle James and Aunt Mary had not shown any great enthusiasm for her when I arrived with her, but I assured myself that they were basically kind and when they knew I'd gone they'd feed her.

I leaned down and ran my hand down her back. A loud purr rattled in her. She opened her blue eyes. "Sammy, Sammy," I whispered. "I wouldn't do this except I have to make sure my baby's all right."

Samantha gave a grunt and rolled on her back as an inducement to rub her tummy. I rubbed it, and for a moment almost gave up my plan. I couldn't bear the thought of anything happening to her, or of her being neglected. For a second I hesitated. Then I saw a small piece of newspaper sticking out of the bottom drawer, and I knew I'd have to trust my uncle and aunt to be good to Samantha. I had to go.

I stuffed my shoulder bag with anything I might need, and made sure I had my bank card. There was, I knew, a money dispensing machine at the terminal where I could use my card and get some funds.

Every now and then I paused to listen just in case Uncle James had decided to come up and chat. But the television was on downstairs and catching a sentence every here and there, I realized it was the kind of documentary he liked.

Praying it would last, I forced myself to wait. I put on jeans, sneakers, a sweater and a zip jacket. At nine-thirty I heard him go into the kitchen and come back into the living room. Probably, I thought, he went for a beer. Neither my uncle nor aunt was what you'd call a drinker, but Uncle James did like a beer as the evening wore on. The time to go was now.

I leaned down and put my face against Samantha's side and kissed her. "I'll be back, I promise you," I whispered.

The stairs were carpeted and I was able to get down and through the small hall to the kitchen without making any sound.

Getting my bike from the garage was no problem. Making sure I had the chain and padlock in the basket, I wheeled it down the drive and then took off down the street.

I could, of course, check the bike at the checking place in the bus terminal, but that would mean that my aunt and uncle would know all the sooner where I'd gone, and probably find out what bus I had taken. So, with a sigh and a conviction that that was the last time I'd see it, I put it in the bike stand outside the building and chained it to one of the stanchions. I knew enough to realize that that wouldn't stop anybody who could pick the lock or cut the chain, but there was nothing more I could do. Then I went to the cash dispensing machine and got enough to get me to Boston, and some over. I was glad to see that there were half a dozen people in front of the ticket window, which made it less likely that the man behind the counter would remember me clearly. Even so, I put on some dark glasses and kept my face down as I said gruffly, "Boston, one way."

"You'll have to change in New York," he said laconically. Look at the departure schedule there."

That was all right with me. I'd been in New York often, and I knew the Port Authority terminal was so huge there was even less of a chance that anyone would remember me.

An hour later the bus pulled into the terminal on Eighth Avenue. I'd heard about the Port Authority—how there were pimps all over the place waiting to approach any girl who got off a bus from the boonies, offering her somewhere to stay and a helping hand, and before she knew what she was doing, she was on the streets. So I was almost disappointed when no one came up to me in the hour I waited before taking the bus to Boston. In fact, I'd have welcomed some kind of interruption, because I found myself thinking about Samantha, suddenly afraid that Uncle James and Aunt Mary wouldn't think to look after her or feed her. And if she were unhappy, mightn't she wander out into the street, looking for me, a street where there was always a fair amount of traffic . . . ?

The picture of what might happen was suddenly so vivid I felt sick with fear, astonished I'd feel so passionately about an animal. To get my mind off Samantha, I made myself think about some of the accounts of the abuse to children I'd read in the various newspapers I'd picked up. And, of course, the fear was back, only much greater, because this time it would be my baby.

"Are you okay?" I jumped and stared at the speaker, a middle-aged man who was waiting in the same line for the same bus I was.

"Fine," I said, reminding myself that pimps could just as easily appear to be middle-aged middle-class men in business suits as the gaudier types with gold chains that usually were described in the more lurid accounts I'd read about young girls who get picked up. "Thank you," I finished, and turned my back.

I glanced at my watch. It was now eleven-thirty. Aunt Mary would be home. Would she look into my room? Most likely not, since she said she'd see me tomorrow morning. What would happen then to Samantha? Would she feed her?

My mind slid off abused children and stuck again on my cat. I dug in my pocket and collected all the change I had. All I had to say was, please feed Samantha and make sure she doesn't go out, and hang up. They wouldn't know where I was calling from, or would they? My worry over Samantha and my need to get to Boston warred in me. Still battling it out inside, I turned to the man who had spoken to me. "Would you please hold my place for me?" I asked.

"I thought you'd decided I was a white slaver," the man said.

I couldn't help it—worried as I was, I giggled a little. "Will you?"

There were pay phones halfway down the long hall. Unfortunately, they were all in use, and I stood impatiently waiting for one of the talkers to release a phone. Finally one came free. I walked over, put a quarter into the slot and started to dial. Then I saw, far down the hall, the line I'd been in begin to move. I ran, dodging people, knocking into others. Just as I reached it, the man who was guarding my place went through the door.

"Excuse me," I said to the woman behind him. "He was holding my place for me."

"First come, first served," she said. "Go to the end of the line."

"No." The man turned around. "She's with me."

The woman glared at me as I slipped through the door. "Thanks," I said to the man as I got into the bus behind him.

"My pleasure."

I had resigned myself to the certainty that I'd now have to sit beside him all the way to Boston. But as I got into one double seat, he nodded and continued to the back.

During the four-and-a-half-hour ride to Boston my mind kept sliding between how to find Trudy Shannon and whether Samantha would be taken care of. A tabloid being read across the aisle that sported the headline NEW REVELATIONS ABOUT CHILD ABUSE didn't help, either.

Maybe it was because of that I couldn't sleep. The seat next to me was empty when we pulled out of New York, and I was just feeling good about that when at the bus's next stop, someone got on and sat down. He was an enormously fat man who bulged into my seat both over and under the arm in the middle. The moment the bus started off again he put his head back. In a few minutes his mouth fell open and snores emerged. He also had bad breath.

I turned toward the window and decided I'd try to sleep myself. But his elbow stuck into my back and pressed steadily until I had to shift.

A voice above my head said, "There's an empty seat beside me. Would you like to sit there?" It was the man who had held my place for me.

"Thanks," I said. Getting past the snoring sleeper was no easy task. Finally the man standing shook the sleeper by the shoulder. "The girl has to get out. Please get up and let her by." His voice wasn't loud, but there was something about it that made the man wake up.

Grumbling and creaking, he moved. I slid past, reached up to the rack above for my pack and followed my rescuer to two seats back.

"Better a white slaver than a snoring monster, right?" There was an ironic note in his voice.

"Yes," I said. Then, before I could think where the statement would lead, I said, "I didn't think you were a white slaver. I'm not even sure what that is."

"That's a giveaway of my age and generation. It's an expression used to describe a man who lures girls somewhere not for their own good."

"Oh," I said. "Well, I did think you might be a pimp."

He closed his eyes. "I'm sorry I brought it up."

Again, I giggled. "Are you sorry you rescued me?"

"Yes. At least for the moment."

We rode in silence for a while. I could still see the headline in the scandal sheet from where I sat.

"Do you live in Boston?" I asked.

"No. Well, a part of greater Boston. I live in Cambridge."

"Harvard," I said gloomily. My father had gone there and I knew it was a good university, but I didn't think anyone there would be a help in trying to find a Trudy Shannon.

"You look disappointed. Would it be better if I had said Yale?"

"But that's in New Haven."

"True."

My mind was still working on whether he could help me locate Trudy. "Do you know anything about how to locate somebody in a city when you don't know their name or address?"

"Well, only the usual references—missing persons, and so on. Is the—er—person you're looking for missing?"

"No. She lived there, at least she did a year ago."

"Have you tried the phone book?"

"Of course." I paused, reluctant to go on to the next step, which would be to give Trudy's name. "But there are lots of names in the phone book that could be her name—I mean by initial and so on."

We rode in silence for a while. Then he said, "The only thing I can suggest is that you think of everything else you know about her and anyone she ever mentioned and see if you can work up a connection there." He looked down at me. "Like, what kind of work she did, or what school she went to, or what neighborhood she might have talked about, or what friend's name she might have mentioned."

What did I know about Trudy other than the fact that like me she was pregnant? The trouble was, she arrived only shortly before I left. Did she say anything about the man who had been the father? I thought carefully. No.

66

Other than saying she was angry, nothing. Did she say anything about her parents? Something flickered in my mind. I tried to go back and catch it. But it was no use. And then whatever it was flickered again. There was something, something set off by the man's question, but no matter how much I tried to back up and repeat the moment, I couldn't focus on what it was. Was there anything else?

No, I decided after some more miles had gone by. There was nothing. Without my willing it, my mind slid to where my baby was and with whom and what might be happening to him. Which brought me back to wishing I could remember what it was Trudy had said, so that I could find her, and if I found her I might be able to locate my baby. It all seemed to hang on that one frail hook. . . .

I stared out the dark window. The highway was lighted, of course, but the countryside beyond it was black. Then I thought about Samantha. Her litter box was in my bathroom, so she could get to it all right, even though I had closed the door on her. Would she cry, in that loud, plaintive voice of hers, attracting Aunt Mary's attention? What might happen if—and I heard again in my imagination the screeching brakes of a car traveling too fast in a residential area.

I must have made a sound. Then I looked down and saw my hands twisting the cords of the pack I'd taken off my back. I had tried to shove it under my seat this time, but I was still holding the straps.

"Whatever it is, I hope you find what you're looking for. Or should I hope that?"

I glanced up at the man's face. There was a quizzical look on it, but also concern. "Do you have any daughters?" I asked.

"Two, and a son. One of my daughters is around your age, about sixteen? Seventeen? Is that right?"

I debated saying eighteen, which would make me an adult, but maybe he'd be more careful if he knew I was a minor around his daughter's age. "I'm seventeen," I said.

"Are you running away?"

"No. I'm going to visit my aunt." If he thought someone were meeting me, he'd be less liable to think I could be picked up.

"I see. You travel late for a seventeen-year-old girl visiting her aunt."

"She works during the day," I improvised. "It's easier for her to meet me at night."

"I see."

I knew he didn't believe me. And what was I going to do when we arrived? Rush up to a strange woman?

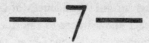

— 7 —

I continued to shift between my anxiety over my baby and my anxiety over Samantha during the next hour until finally, I drifted off to sleep.

"Wake up!" a voice said beside me.

I opened my eyes and found the bus had stopped moving.

"We're in Boston," the man said. He was standing in the aisle, his bag in his hand.

I got up and pulled my backpack from beneath my seat. "Go ahead," I said, hoping he'd just take off and not wait around to see me greeted by my fictitious aunt.

When we got out and into the main part of the terminal I stood there for a minute, pretending I was looking for somebody.

The man, who had walked a few paces ahead of me, came back. "Don't be scared. I'm not trying to pick you up. I don't believe your aunt is meeting you, but that's your business. Here is my card. If you run into trouble or need help and don't know anybody else, call me. In the meantime, if you don't have a place to stay, you might try this," and he scribbled on the back of the card. "Good luck!" He picked up his bag and walked out.

When he'd gone I looked at the back of the card. It read: ST. MONICA'S RESIDENCE, followed by an address and phone number.

I'd had enough of girls' residences of any kind. And if I went there, he'd know where to find me. I had no idea what his intentions might be, but I knew this: if they were bad, I didn't want him to know where I was, and if they were too good, I didn't want it either. I slipped the card into my pocket. Then I looked at my watch. It was ten minutes past five. What I wanted more than anything else was to lie down on a bed and sleep, but I didn't think walking up to a motel at this point would be a good idea. There was a sort of all-night counter in the terminal, so I went there, put my bag under a table, and got a sandwich and some coffee. I also got a newspaper.

An hour later I had drunk three coffees and read the paper from front to back. There were no accounts of children being abused, but there was an ad in the classified section that I tore out and put in my pocket. It said: Looking for somebody? Let us help you. We're experts at finding missing persons, whether children or adults. The address, of course, meant nothing to me. I glanced at my watch. It was now six-thirty. Nobody would be open at six-thirty in the morning. What I needed first was a cheap hotel or motel where I could leave my bag. For a minute I thought about St. Monica's Residence, and then dismissed it. They'd probably tell the police about me.

I waited until eight, taking up the time by reading two more papers, including the ads, and visiting the ladies room, where I did a sort of spot wash.

Finally at eight I went up to a woman at the ticket counter and asked her if she knew of an inexpensive place I could stay.

She looked at me. "How inexpensive?"

"Very."

She thought for a minute. Then she wrote something down. "This is a sort of rooming house. It's not fancy. You'll have to share the bath on the floor." She paused. "A cousin of mine used to run it. Somebody else runs it now. No guarantees." She handed me the paper with an address written on it.

"How do I get there?"

"Give me back the paper. I'll write it out."

When she finished she handed it back to me. "When you get out of the terminal, turn right, then right again, go straight ahead and you'll find the bus I have down there about three blocks on. Or, if you want the subway, I've written down how to get there and what station to get out at."

"Thanks." I took the paper. "Thanks very much."

"Good luck, kid. Be careful."

It was a beautiful day. I turned right and started to walk. By now my uncle and aunt would almost certainly have missed me, because I should have been down for breakfast half an hour ago. I felt a pang of conscience. My mind shifted to Samantha, but I knew that I had to find my baby first, so I forced myself to think about where I was going.

It took me forty-five minutes to arrive at the address the woman at the bus terminal had written down. It turned out to be a plain brick row house in a grungy street. A woman was sitting at the desk in the hall, on which was a phone, a Rolodex, and an open book. "Yes?" she said.

"I'd like a room."

"How'd you find out about this place?"

I hesitated. The woman at the bus terminal seemed

friendly and trustworthy, but there was something sharp and vaguely disquieting about the woman here.

"We don't just take anybody off the street," the woman said. Her dark eyes, narrow in a narrow face, stared at me.

"The woman in the bus terminal gave it to me. She said her cousin used to run it."

"Yeah, well, she did. Now I do." And she laughed. "All right. There's a room empty two floors above. That'll be fifteen dollars a night, in advance."

I took out the bills I had gotten from the cash machine, and as I did, the plastic charge I'd used fell out onto the floor. I stooped over, but she was quicker. Bending, her hand went out and she picked the card up, looking at the name on it. "Claudia Ransom," she said.

"May I have it back, please?"

"Why don't I just keep it while you're here?" She was smiling, but I didn't like the malicious look it gave her.

"Please give it back to me," I repeated, holding out my hand. She didn't move. "Or I'll take this." Before she knew what I was doing, I picked up the Rolodex from her desk and held it beside me. I probably should have taken the book, I thought, but I grabbed the nearest object. Evidently, though, I was right.

"Put that back," she said.

"When you give me back my card."

For a moment we stared at one another. I started to glance at some of the names on the Rolodex.

"Here!" She all but threw the card at me. I picked it up, tossed the Rolodex back on her desk, snatched up my shoulder bag and left quickly. When I got outside I heard the door open again and the woman's voice screeching something at me. I started to run, turning corners here and there as I came to them. Finally I ran out of breath and stopped. Standing there in the cool sunlight, I suddenly felt so tired I could hardly stand up. A taxi came by and the temptation was too great. I got in.

"Where to, lady?"

He had a kind face, but then so did the woman in the bus terminal. I hesitated. He turned.

"I want to go to a motel, not too expensive, but okay."

He stared at me in the rearview mirror. "You a runaway?"

"No. Anyway, I'm eighteen. I have the right to do anything I want."

"Okay."

"Near the bus terminal," I said quickly. I didn't want to be in some section of Boston I didn't know the way out of.

"I can take you to a hotel or motel near the terminal, but it ain't that cheap, or I can take you to one that is, but it ain't anyplace I'd like a gal of mine to be in. You follow?"

"Yes," I said. Then, despite my anxiety, I gave a huge yawn.

He laughed. "Okay. I'll take you to one I think'll be okay."

When the taxi stopped we were in front of a motel that didn't look too expensive or run-down.

I stared at the meter and pulled a few bills from my pocket, carefully not letting my plastic card drop again. "Here," I said, handing over some money. "I hope that tip's okay."

"It's fine. Look. It ain't my business. But that wasn't such a great section I picked you up in. Do you know Boston?"

73

I thought about lying but decided not to. "No."

"Well, the bus terminal is about three blocks that way and two blocks to the right of that. You're young and you're good-looking. You ought to be careful."

Somehow what he said made me think of the man in the bus. Maybe I ought to look into that residence he'd written down. "Thanks," I said, and got out of the taxi.

I was half expecting the people at the motel desk to want to know who I was and what I was doing, but the man merely turned the book around for my signature. I'd already made up in my mind a fake name and address. I wrote "Barbara Hunt" and gave the actual street address, but not the name, of the school in Vermont. The man turned the book around, glanced at what I had written and handed over a key.

My room was on the second floor. When I got in I double-locked the door and drew aside the curtain, to find I was looking out on a parking lot and more buildings. But it felt safe. Dropping my bag on the floor, I pulled down the cover on the bed and sank onto it.

I woke up and for a few seconds wondered where I was. Then I saw the parking lot through the window and the television set in the room and remembered. I looked at my watch. It was almost six o'clock. I had slept nearly ten hours. Which meant that it was now evening. I was also extremely hungry. And I had to think up a way to find Trudy Shannon. I swung my feet onto the floor and sat there, fighting a sense of depression and hopelessness. Then I thought about my baby, and all the stories I had read came crowding into my head. It didn't matter how I felt, I had to find him.

I took a shower, changed my underclothes and shirt and

went downstairs. On the far side of the lobby were some glass doors and a sign, DINING ROOM, over them. But places marked Dining Room were usually expensive. What I needed was a diner or coffee shop. I left the motel, turned right, and started to walk. Sure enough, after half a block I found a coffee shop and went in.

As I sat eating my burger and cole slaw, I considered my options. Then I remembered the ad in the paper I had seen. Getting it out of my pocket, I went over to a pay phone against the far wall and called the number. What I got was an answering tape, and realized that of course it was now seven-thirty and long after office hours.

So where did that leave me?

Maybe a different paper would have a different ad. "Where can I get a newspaper?" I asked the man behind the counter.

"At the corner. Wanna look at this one? Somebody left it behind." He opened it up and then stopped, staring at it. "Hey, that's you, isn't it?" He held it up.

There, on the front page, was my picture, one taken by the school. "Claudia Ransom, seventeen, missing," read the headline.

I looked up and found both countermen and a couple of customers looking at me.

"You ought to be ashamed of yourself," a woman's voice said beside me.

I turned and looked at her. She was middle-aged and disapproving.

"Why?" I said. "And why is it your business?"

"Worrying your family like that," she said.

"Maybe she has a good reason, a girl said from the other side of the counter. Maybe she was ill treated."

"That's what you kids always claim, whether it's true or not," the woman shot back.

At that point the girl snapped out something else. It was weird. They were talking about me as though I weren't there.

"You ought to at least call them," an older man with an apron said.

"Is there a reward?" I don't know who said that, but I decided it was time I got out of there.

"Here," I said, and put some bills down on the counter. Before anybody knew what I was doing, I walked out.

I was walking toward the motel when I realized that by this time probably the people there would know I had run away. Motels often had newspaper counters. I hesitated, then turned into a block away from the motel. I knew I had to find a newspaper myself to see what it said.

I found a newsstand two blocks down, then went into another coffee shop, ordered some coffee, and, keeping the picture hidden, read the news account.

Because I was still, technically, a minor, the police had already started to search and Uncle James and Aunt Mary had given the newspapers the picture. And then it hit me like a clap of thunder that my parents would probably know now, too. Even if my uncle and aunt hadn't called them in Europe, the police might have and, anyway, I knew from living there, American papers can be bought in any reasonably sized city.

I hadn't even thought about that.

Suddenly my mind focused on Samantha and I wanted to cry. Why with her, especially, I didn't know. But I felt my eyes fill. And then I realized I thought about her because I couldn't bear to think about my baby.

At that point, as though in some kind of horror movie,

a child near me started to cry. I jumped and swung around. There was a baby in a pram near me. A girl at the table next to me, reading a magazine, put out her hand and started jiggling the carriage. The baby went on crying. "Oh, shut up," the girl said, turning a page in her magazine. "I'll feed you in a minute."

She looked even younger than me. Her blond hair was frizzed up and on top of her head. The baby went on wailing. I tried not to think about it. Instead, I thought about everything I had read about how babies could drive even the best mother nuts, but as soon as my mind worked on that, I saw that it just made me feel worse faster, so I pulled my mind away and tried to think again about Samantha. To distract me, I picked up the paper again and concentrated on the pages I hadn't read. The baby went on crying, not as loud now, but in a sort of desolate way that was worse.

"Why don't you feed it or hug it or something?" I suddenly heard myself say to the girl.

"Who the hell are you?" she said.

There was silence all around.

"Maybe it needs a bottle," I said after a minute, trying to sound concerned instead of angry.

"It'll get a bottle when we get home!"

And then, as though it had been programmed and I had pushed the right button, my mind went to supposing it were my baby with a mother who was already sorry she'd adopted it sitting here wishing it would shut up. . . .

I glanced up to see the girl and everybody in the diner staring at me. Had they seen my picture?

I got up quickly and was walking out, when the man behind the counter said, "You haven't paid for your coffee."

"Sorry!" I mumbled.

"Minds other people's business but tries to steal her own coffee," the loving young mother said, still jiggling the carriage.

I walked back, put a dollar on the counter and then left. Had they seen my picture? I didn't know. I started back toward the motel when I realized that if the man who checked me in hadn't seen my picture, maybe somebody else had. I could walk back into the arms of the police, then I could kiss any idea of finding my baby good-bye.

I stopped where I was and realized, as though for the first time, that it was now dark. I looked both to the left and the right. I couldn't go back to the motel, not without risking getting caught. So what could I do? All my life I'd read about kids who'd run away from home, gone to the nearest bus terminal, taken a ticket to the closest city, and then disappeared. It all sounded so easy. I wished I hadn't spent all day in bed. At least if it were light that missing persons place would be open.

"Hey, how about a date?"

I whirled around. He was large and gross. When I saw his hand coming at me I ran. I ran about three blocks, turning corners to keep him from coming after me. Now I found I was facing some kind of park. I could go in there, but even I knew a park was not a place for a girl to go by herself at night. To my right was what looked like a large, very expensive hotel. Hotels had lobbies. I looked down at my jeans and sneakers. It didn't matter, I told myself. Everybody wore them now. I waited until the doorman went to open a car, then I walked quickly in, went straight to the lobby, and sat down, opening the paper in front of me but making sure that the page carrying my picture wasn't showing.

Nobody approached me. After a while I relaxed and lowered the paper a little, so I could see over it. Straight ahead was a rank of phones. I wasn't even tempted to call my uncle and aunt. I felt bad about their worry, and I'd give a lot to ask them please to feed Samantha, but if they could find me, that would be the end of trying to locate my baby.

But the phones mesmerized me. After a minute I dug in my pocket for the card the man had given me. It still said "St. Monica's Residence" on one side. I turned it over.

On the other side it said in square letters in the middle, "Charles Patterson." Then, down to one side, "Fairbairn Residence, Cambridge."

I found myself walking toward the phones before I even realized what I was going to do. Calling information, I got the number for Fairbairn Residence and dialed.

— 8 —

I don't know what I expected. My heart was beating so hard I could hardly hear the man's voice. "Fairbairn Residence."

"May I speak to Charles Patterson."

"Whom shall I say is calling?"

I should have foreseen that. I was about to hang up when I suddenly remembered something he'd said. "A friend of his daughter's," I said.

"Oh." The man's voice sounded much friendlier. "Just a minute, please."

In a few seconds the voice I recognized came over. "This is Charles Patterson. Now, are you Nancy's or Debbie's friend?"

I took a breath. "I'm sorry, Mr. Patterson. I didn't want to give my own name. I'm—I'm the girl you gave your card to in the bus terminal this morning. And I'm in—I thought maybe you could give me some advice." It sounded not only lame and wimpy, but like some kind of con game.

"Advice about what?"

Even after all that sleep a feeling of tiredness hit me

again. How much farther could I run without somebody somewhere helping me?

"Are you in trouble?" he asked.

"Sort of."

I had a sudden fear that he was going to hang up. But then why did he give me his card?"

"You'd better come here and tell me about it. Do you know how to get to Cambridge?"

"No."

"Where are you?"

"In a big hotel."

"Which hotel?"

"Opposite a sort of park."

"The Ritz-Carlton?"

"I don't know."

"Look toward the desk. Is there anything there with the name Ritz-Carlton or the letters RC on it?"

I looked over to the desk. There I could see a stand with some notepaper. On the notepaper was some printing. "Just a minute," I said, and ran over. Then I came back. "Yes, it says Ritz-Carlton."

"All right. Do you have enough money for a taxi to Cambridge? You'll need about ten or twelve dollars."

"Yes."

"Take a taxi. Ask the doorman to tell the taxi to drive you to this address." And he gave me a street number in Cambridge.

"Shouldn't I just get in a taxi and give the driver the number."

"You could. But if the doorman does it, the driver is more certain to drive you here safely and not try anything with an obviously young and pretty stranger in the city."

"All right."

"I'll expect you in about half an hour."

As I rode along, looking at the Charles River, I thought, I'd trusted Alan Huntly too. And he seemed as kind and well bred as this man. But I knew that by myself I couldn't go any further.

The first shock was the man who opened the door to the rather handsome house the taxi stopped at.

He was wearing a cassock. He stepped back. "Come in."

I was shown into a large room with big chairs, a wall filled with books and a fireplace.

"Well now, what trouble are you in?"

The man from the bus was standing there. The thing that made my jaw drop was that he was wearing a black suit and a round collar.

"You're a priest!"

"Yes."

"But—but you said you had children!"

"I do. I am also a widower. I came into the Church after my wife died and my children were grown. Why don't you sit down?"

"Then why weren't you wearing that—that collar on the bus?"

He smiled a little. "There's no rule about it. Obviously you feel deceived."

I stood there for a moment, then sat down. All I could think about was, if I left here, where would I go? Still, the religiousness of the principal in Vermont loomed large in my mind.

"I suppose you're terribly religious and moral," I said.

"You make them sound like a particularly revolting disease."

I giggled a little.

·"Tell me about it," he said gently.

"I had a baby. He'd be four months old now. My parents—well, Mother wanted me to . . . well, to get rid of it, but I didn't want to, so they sent me up to a school for unwed mothers in Vermont where they put bastards"—I threw the word out—"up for adoption." I hesitated, then the rest fell out. "A while ago I read about a child who was killed in New York by the people who adopted her, and the adopted boy was found bruised and neglected, and then every time I looked at a paper I saw more stories about children being abused—especially children who didn't seem to belong to anybody, and I tried to find out where my baby had been adopted just so I could know he was all right, but they'd never tell me officially at the school, and the only two people who might help me have disappeared. One of them, a girl who was with me there— her name's Trudy Shannon—came from Boston, and I thought she might know where the one teacher who was nice had gone. So that's why I came to Boston. But there're lots of Shannons in Boston . . ." My voice seemed to run down of its own accord.

"There are indeed. You couldn't tell your parents about this? Your mother?"

Any faint hope that he'd just help me without asking questions vanished. But where could I go? Where could I get any other help? "I don't want to talk about who I am," I said stubbornly.

Then he surprised me. "All right. I take it you want to talk about your problem, finding Trudy Shannon."

"Yes."

"I'll drive a bargain with you. I'll do my best to help you to find Trudy Shannon if you will let me take you to St. Monica's Residence where it is safe for you to stay."

83

I opened my mouth to say, But my backpack's in the motel, when I suddenly realized where that would lead to. "All right," I said. I could buy a toothbrush.

"Were you going to say something?"

I shook my head. "No."

"Let me call St. Monica's. Then I'll come back and we'll tackle the subject of Trudy Shannon."

He came back carrying a tray with a pot, two cups and a plate with a sandwich on it. "It occurred to me you might be hungry."

I wasn't hungry, I thought, but the coffee looked good.

He put the tray down on a table next to me, poured two cups of coffee, filled one of them with milk, then went and sat in the chair opposite.

"Thanks." I bit into the sandwich and suddenly realized I was hungrier than I thought. Between bites I asked, "Did St. Monica's head person say they had room?" I didn't think there was a danger—or hope—she'd turn me down, but I was also wondering if she had read the evening paper and would ask him if I could be the missing girl.

"Oh, yes. And I could be biased, but I don't think she'll come over to you as repellently religious or moral." He looked at me for a moment. I kept my attention on my sandwich.

"How old was this Trudy Shannon? Your age, seventeen?"

"Actually, she was younger than me. She was just sixteen, but she looked older because she was bigger."

He was frowning. "That's horribly young to have an unwanted pregnancy. Do you have any idea who the father was?"

"No. But—"

"But what?"

Something jiggled in my mind again. "She said something about it being a member of the family."

His brows drew down over his nose. "That's truly ugly. So she was probably fifteen when it happened." He paused. "With a name like Shannon, and coming from Boston, it's a fair bet she was Irish or of Irish descent. I could make inquiries from some of the parish priests. They'd be the most likely to know. Except—" He stopped.

"Except what?"

He got up. "There are several homes or houses for unwed mothers here in the city, many of them run by nuns. I could start there. By the way, how old would her baby be now? I mean, when would she have delivered it?"

"Maybe a month ago."

"All right. She's now sixteen and big. Can you describe her any more closely?"

I thought how she looked, sitting across the table from me at the school. "Well, she was pregnant, so I don't know now whether she'd be fat or thin. She had reddish-brown curly hair, freckles, greenish eyes and teeth that stuck out a little in front."

He smiled. "Are you politely saying buck teeth?"

"I liked her. So I can't say she had buck teeth. They weren't unattractive. They just stuck out a little."

"All right. Ready?"

"Yes."

"What happened to your backpack?"

That would open up a whole other can of worms. "I lost it." I was surprised at how bad I felt lying to this man who was helping me. But I made myself think about my baby. Making sure he was all right came before anything.

He was looking at me. I could feel the heat coming up into my face.

"I suppose it's to your credit that you're a bad liar. That was a lie, wasn't it?"

"Yes. I'm sorry."

We stood there.

He said. "I'm sure St. Monica's will have a toothbrush."

We went in his car, driving through streets with nice row houses.

"Where's Harvard?" I asked.

"Scattered around. I'll point out some of the better-known buildings." And he did.

Finally we drew up outside a plain row house in a pleasant street. The windows were lit. My heart started beating. Suddenly I was afraid that when the door opened I'd see policemen lined up.

"What's the matter? No one's going to hurt you."

For a moment just running seemed a wonderful idea. But where? For the last two days I had run away and kept running. And I was no nearer finding where my baby was.

"What are you afraid of?" he asked again.

"Are they going to call the police?"

"Nobody will call the police without your permission. And in case your mind is running in that direction, nobody will force you to give it. All right?"

I nodded. He started up the steps to the front door, letting me follow. It was that small act of trust that enabled me to climb the steps after him.

He rang the bell. The door was opened almost immediately. A tall girl stood there with her back to the light. I couldn't see her face well. But it didn't matter.

"Trudy!" I cried. "It's you!"

"Claudia," she said. "Claudia Ransom!"

— 9 —

She came down the steps and hugged me. I hugged her back, even though she'd given my name away to Father Patterson and to the woman in a nun's habit who now stood in the doorway.

"It's all right," he said. "I had a feeling you might be Claudia Ransom."

"You read the paper."

"No, I listened to the radio."

"Are you going to tell the police?"

"I'd like to call your family, at least, to let them know you're all right."

"They'll make me come back and not try to find my baby."

"If I promise to do everything I can to help you find your baby, will you call your family?"

I thought about it. I didn't want to call my family. Why I felt so strongly about it I wasn't sure. At least, though, I could remind them about Samantha. "All right," I said reluctantly.

"I know how I'd feel if you were my daughter."

"It's hard to think about a priest having a daughter," I said. It sounded grudging. But I felt grudging.

"I know. Would you feel I was more authentic if I told you that Cardinal Manning of London was married before going into the Church?"

They took me in and to a room where there was a phone. "It's long distance," I said, and then realized they'd know that.

"That's all right." And they left me alone with the telephone. Finally I picked up the receiver and dialed and stood, listening to the rings.

It was Uncle James who answered.

"This is Claudia," I said.

"Where the hell are you?"

"In Cambridge, staying in a nun's residence. So you needn't worry about that."

"How did you get there?"

"How's Samantha?" I asked instead. "Did you feed her?"

"Yes, of course we fed her. What do you think we are? Monsters who starve pets?"

I suddenly realized he was hurt as well as angry. "I'm sorry, Uncle James," I said. "But when I read all those stories about that girl who was adopted and who was beaten to death and the boy who was adopted with her, and others, I had to find out if my baby's all right."

"Why didn't you ask us to help you? I know some people in Vermont and could have maybe pulled some strings."

"But you didn't know about me having a baby."

"We sure as hell do now. We had a long, expensive transatlantic conversation with your parents. Here's your aunt."

"Claudia, how are you?" Aunt Mary said. I'd always thought of Uncle James as more sympathetic and understanding than Aunt Mary, but her voice was so kind it made me want to cry.

"I'm all right," I said, swallowing. "I guess you know now all about . . . about me having a baby."

"Yes."

"Maybe I should have told you, but—"

"I think I'd have felt the way you did. Are you trying to locate the baby now?"

"Yes. I just want to make sure it's all right. I've been reading all those horrible stories about children, adopted children, who've been abused, and so on."

"Won't the principal of that school tell you, if you explain to her?"

"You don't understand what she's like. She thinks we're all wicked girls who should be punished. If she knew I was trying to find out who the people were who adopted my baby, she'd do everything she could to warn them and to keep me from knowing."

There was a pause at the other end of the phone. Then: "What are your present plans?"

"I was trying to find the girl here in Boston I was at the school with. I know it's crazy, but when I walked into this place, St. Monica's Residence, she was here."

"And is she able to help you?"

"I haven't talked to her yet. I thought she might know where the one teacher I liked was. She's left the school and nobody there seems to know where she is. I thought she might know how to get into the right file or something."

"Well, good luck. Let us know if you need anything. Do you have enough money, by the way?"

They were being so kind, I felt awful. "I'm fine," I said.

Uncle James said, "Samantha's fine, too."

"I know you're feeding her."

"Of course we are. But she misses you. She goes around the house crying and looking for you."

I felt a stab of pain and self-reproach. But I had to find my baby. "Give her a pat for me."

"I will. If we want to reach you, can we call the address there? What is it, St. Monica's?"

"Yes." I looked at the phone and saw the number. "It's six one seven, five five five, eight nine four five."

"All right." I heard the phone click at the other end.

For a few minutes I just sat there. Then I went out. Father Patterson and Trudy were standing talking to the nun.

"Everything okay?" he said.

"Yes. They were—I guess I didn't need to run away."

"It's always nice when people turn out better than we feared."

I looked at him, and knew he was laughing.

"Yes, I suppose you're right."

"Now you've found your friend here—"

"Did you know she'd be here?" I asked suddenly. I knew I'd been wondering that.

"You're very suspicious, aren't you? But I have to admit it did cross my mind that if she were in any kind of trouble, this would be one of the logical places for her—certainly with a name like Shannon."

"I guess so."

"It's all right. As I was saying, now that you've found your friend, you can talk to her about your project. I'll speak to you tomorrow."

* * *

"Trudy, I've got to find out if my baby's all right," I said when he'd left and we were alone.

"Lotsa luck," she said.

"What about yours?" I asked, suddenly aware that she probably had her worries, too.

"Mine died," she said abruptly.

It caught me short. "I'm sorry," I said. "What happened?"

"Let's go into the living room and sit down."

I looked at her closely then. She had on jeans and a shirt. She was much thinner than I remembered her, and her face looked older.

"I left that awful place not long after you did, and came back here." She paused. "I couldn't go home, so I went to stay with a friend, but . . . but the friend's mother told my mother that I was there, and she and . . . and her husband turned up with the police. I saw them coming from the upstairs window, so I ran downstairs and jumped out of the window at the back and ran down the street. I managed to get away." She stopped.

"What happened then?"

"Oh, God, Claudia, I got in with some street people. I started taking drugs and got involved in other . . . in other things. Then one night I fell and passed out. When I woke up I was in the hospital. They told me I'd had a miscarriage. I thought I'd be glad to lose the brat, because, well, I thought I would, but I wasn't. A social worker came to see me and started talking about a foster home because I was still underage, so I ran away again when the nurses weren't watching. Somebody told me about this place— it's for runaway girls and is a sort of halfway house. That's when I came here. Sister MacNeill is nice."

"I'm sorry, Trudy. Really." I reached out and took her hand, and we sat there for a bit.

"What happened to Miss Halsey?" I asked. I hated to be thinking in terms of a last hope, but I knew that's what she was.

"The Prune? She got canned soon after you left."

"Why?"

"Who knows? Old Gaitskill probably thought she was too nice to the girls, didn't have the right punishing attitude toward them."

"Do you know where she went?"

Trudy shook her head. "Sorry! I was in the middle of troubles of my own and didn't pay much attention."

I sat there, knowing the last of my hope had gone.

After a minute the door opened and the nun came in. "I've put you in Trudy's room, Claudia. I thought you might like to be with her."

"Come on, let's go upstairs," Trudy said.

As we went up I asked, "If this is a halfway house, where are all the other girls?"

"In the annex next door. The nuns sleep in this building and there's an extra bedroom here which they gave me because the annex was full. The rest of the residence—the rooms, the dining and recreational and classrooms—are over there, through the door leading from the downstairs hall." We reached the top and walked down the hall. "Here we are," Trudy said.

It was a medium-size room with two beds, a bureau and a closet. "The bath's to your right down the hall," Trudy explained. "Don't you have any bag?"

I told her about the motel. "It's there, but I'm afraid to go back. Probably by this time they've caught on to who

93

I am and I'll find the police there." I hesitated. "Do you think you could get me a toothbrush?"

"Sure."

She left the room and returned in a few minutes. "Here's a toothbrush. You can use my toothpaste, and here's an extra-long T-shirt you can use as a nightgown. And here are some pants I got out of the all-purpose closet in the hall. You're small and they look like they might fit."

When we were lying in bed, I said, "Trudy, what are you going to do when you get out of here?"

"I don't know. Sister MacNeill's said something about getting me some kind of scholarship to a community school and junior college."

"Would you like that?"

"Yeah. What I want more than anything is to be able to get a halfway decent job and live by myself and be independent. But for that I need an education."

"What . . . what about your parents?"

There was always something about her voice when she talked about them that made me realize she might not want to answer. But I asked anyway.

"I don't have any."

"I thought—"

"There's a woman who calls herself my mother. Maybe she is. But since she gave me to her current so-called husband to play around with I don't want to see her ever again."

That explained some of the things she said. "Was he—?" I started tentatively.

"Yes. Let's not talk about it."

"Okay. I'm sorry."

* * *

I went to sleep right away, but suddenly I was in a room and there was a woman there I recognized as Miss Gait-skill. She had a stick in her hand and was beating a small boy, who was crying and holding his hands over his face. "More, more," a man said, standing there and watching. She raised the stick. The child screamed.

"No, no, no," I cried, and then found whoever was trying to hit the little boy was gripping and shaking me. I screamed.

"Wake up! Wake up, Claudia!"

I opened my eyes and saw Trudy, holding my shoulders. In back of her was the nun.

"That was a bad one, wasn't it," the nun said.

"I dreamed she was trying to kill my baby."

"It was a dream," Trudy said. "Just a dream!" Her hair was rumpled and she was in her nightgown.

"Are you all right?" the nun asked. She was in a robe, I noticed.

"What time is it?"

"About three A.M.?"

I let out my breath. "I was dreaming, wasn't I?"

"Of course."

"I'm sorry," I said.

"It's all right. Do you think you can go back to sleep?"

"Yes," I said.

The nun left and Trudy got back into bed and turned off the light that was above her.

I stared out the window into the night sky. There was a moon, small and crescent-shaped, visible through the trees that were above the window. It looked like a nice night, and I knew beyond any doubt that I had to get out of there.

Why I was so sure, I didn't know. I told myself that I

95

was in the best possible place. That Father Patterson and my family would try to help me find my baby. The trouble was, I didn't really believe it. Somewhere in the dream I became convinced that my baby was in danger, and if I myself didn't get there right now, he'd be lost to me forever.

The rational part of my mind reminded me that Father Patterson and my family could pull strings and maybe force that evil Miss Gaitskill to tell them where my baby was. But I didn't really believe that, either. And I was desperately afraid that by pulling the strings, they'd just make her more determined than ever. And even if it did work, it would take too long.

And then, oddly, I thought of Alan. Whenever I'd thought of him since I knew I was pregnant, I thought of him with anger and resentment. Now it was as though he were trying to tell me something.

"He's a rotten fink," I told myself.

I slipped out of bed. *You're crazy*, a calmer, saner part of me said in my head. But I went on dressing, taking care to be very quiet about it. Trudy didn't stir. I expected to be stopped by somebody as I crept down the stairs. But nobody stopped me.

I slipped out the front door just as the first light was beginning to show, and I walked quickly until I came across a taxi.

"Bus terminal," I said as I got in.

It was no use my watching the streets to make sure he took me in the right direction, because I didn't know Cambridge. However, at the end of about twenty-five minutes I did recognize the bus terminal. These taxi rides were costing me my precious dollars, I thought, peeling off the fare plus tip.

The next bus to where I wanted to go was at six with a one-hour wait at the other end for a connecting bus. The school was in a small town and buses didn't go there often. So I sat in the now-familiar terminal. Luckily, there was the coffee shop near there, so I was able to get some breakfast. My one fear was that when they woke up at St. Monica's they'd guess where I'd be. But nobody turned up. At ten to six I got on the bus and started to Vermont.

It was nearly four and a half hours later. The bus had come into a terminal in one of Vermont's bigger cities, where I had to wait for the other bus. It had been a long ride. I was tired and anxious and afraid that when the nun found I'd run away she would make Trudy tell her where the school was. It wouldn't take them long to figure out how I'd got there and that I'd have to wait for another bus. Would they then tell the police, or my family, or the school? Would I see police coming through the terminal door to look for me?

At that moment my eyes focused on the name of a college in large white letters on a red sweater worn by a boy who, judging from his age, his backpack, his bookbag, and his hockey stick was almost certainly a college student. That was the college Alan had gone to and was eventually planning to return to to teach.

I stared at the name. Gone was my memory of the night before of his gentleness. What was back was the rage I felt at him. He'd got me into this. I was here, sitting in a strange bus terminal, waiting for another bus, being looked for by the police, all because he got me drunk and . . . and took advantage of me not only by what he did in his apartment, but by not even telling me he was married.

I got up and bought some coffee from a coffee machine.

It tasted vile, as though it had been made three weeks before. There was a candy machine, but the thought of candy made my stomach flip over. I finally settled for a package of plain cookies. Maybe if I ate something I'd feel better.

I didn't. And my anger hadn't abated. It was Alan's fault that my baby could be being mistreated somewhere. It was his fault that Samantha—But Uncle James had said they'd feed Samantha. Even so, she wasn't happy. She was trying to get out to look for me. That was part of the whole misery.

Suddenly a man's voice came over the PA system. The bus I was waiting for would be half an hour late owing to an accident on the turnpike farther north.

It seemed the last straw. I still had lots of change from the night before. And here, at least, the phone booth was empty.

I didn't really think I'd find Alan at the college. According to the place where he was studying for his doctorate, he'd gone to France. He did say he was coming back here. But who knew whether he had? I dropped in the coins, got information and the number of the college.

When somebody answered I asked for him.

"Alan Huntly? He lives off campus," the voice said.

I swallowed. "Could you give me his number, I'm calling long distance."

"Well . . ." she hesitated. "Since it's long distance—" And she read the telephone number to me.

I put in another batch of coins and dialed. Of course, I could get his wife. I found myself wishing she'd answer, and in just what insinuating, damaging way I'd speak to her.

But it was Alan who said, "Hello?"

I took a deep breath. "I just called to tell you what a bastard I think you are. You raped me and got me pregnant and I'm here desperately trying to make sure that my baby's all right and it's all because of you!"

"What the—Claudia?"

"Yes, me, Claudia, the girl you raped."

"I did not rape you. Are you crazy?"

"You made me drunk so I didn't know what I was doing."

"I told you to be careful when you decided to drink my drink as well as yours. And you were entirely willing. Believe me!"

"And what's more, you're married and you didn't even tell me that!"

"I was separated, though it wasn't generally known. Right now my wife is getting a divorce. Where the hell are you?"

"I'm in Rutland, waiting for a bus to take me to the place I went to for unwed mothers, where they took my baby and gave it up for adoption and with everything I've read in the paper he could be horribly mistreated right now." I hadn't meant to cry, but I suddenly burst into tears."

"Listen," Alan said. "Stay where you are. I'm coming to the terminal to talk to you. Stay there!"

"Why should I wait anywhere for you?" I sobbed.

"For God's sake, lady, can't you lower your voice and maybe let somebody else use the phone?"

I turned. There was an angry-looking man immediately behind me and a short line behind him. "Sorry," I mumbled. "Just a minute. Alan—" But the line had been disconnected and there was only a dial tone.

I turned back. Half a dozen faces stared at me. I knew

that when I got upset my voice sometimes went up, but I hadn't meant all of Vermont to learn my business. "Sorry," I muttered again, and went to sit in one of the seats.

I regretted now that I'd called. I didn't want to see Alan again. I hated him. Maybe he wouldn't come. I hoped he wouldn't.

But in forty-five minutes he came through the door. I continued to sit there as he walked toward me. He looked the same, except not quite as tall as I remembered him, and thinner. Also he looked older. I suddenly realized with a shock how much older than me he was.

"Now," he said, sitting down beside me. "What's this about the school and your having a baby?"

I took a breath. "I've told you most of it—I shouted it through the phone."

"You certainly did," he said grimly.

The voice on the PA system sounded again. They were announcing the bus that would take me to the school. I got up. "That's my bus."

"Where are you going?"

I told him the name of the town. "To that school I told you about." I had been furious. Now I was so embarrassed and mortified I wanted to disappear. "That's . . . that's where the baby was adopted from. I have to go."

He got up. "That's only about thirty miles from here. I'll drive you. But . . . I want to talk to you first."

"You don't have to," I said sulkily.

"It's my baby, too—isn't it?"

"Why didn't you tell me you were married?" I asked.

We were sitting in a restaurant. I had been picking at a burger and a salad.

"Because, as I told you, we were separated and I didn't think the marriage was going to—well—get itself together. Also, although you don't sound like you're going to believe it, I didn't plan to—for what happened. And I did not rape you. Let's just get that straight."

"No, but you . . . got me drunk and then took advantage of me."

"I didn't force you to drink. You took what I gave you and drank of your own accord." He paused. "I didn't plan the thing. It just happened. Now, tell me about the baby."

So I told him about the school and Miss Gaitskill and all the horrible stories I'd read about what happened to children.

"Not always," he said. "Lots of adoptions turn out well."

"What about those that don't?"

There was a pause. "You say . . . you said it was a boy?"

"Yes, seven and a half pounds. Black hair. I don't know why. Your hair isn't black and neither's mine."

"I'm told babies often lose the first hair. He looked at me. "You didn't give him a name, did you?"

"No. We were allowed to see the baby once. And then it was taken away for adoption. It had already been spoken for, you see. I didn't want to name it, even to myself. Except—" I stopped.

"Except what?"

"I sometimes thought I'd have called him Alexander. Alex."

There was a sort of silence.

"You know it's better if he was adopted. He'd have two parents."

"That's what everybody says."

"Well, I ought to know. I was adopted."

I looked up at him. "You were?"

"Yes, my parents couldn't have any children, they thought. Then, when they had me, evidently it did something for them, they had my sister in the usual way about three years later."

"Did they make any difference between you and the sister that was born to them?"

"Not a bit. In fact, my sister, when she got mad at me, sometimes said they liked me better."

"A lot of the time I wished I'd kept him."

He didn't say anything. He pulled some money out of his wallet and paid the bill. "We'd better get going if we're to get there this afternoon."

When we got in his car, he said, "You showed me some of the papers you wrote. You write well. You could do something with it. I bet I'm not the first person to tell you that. But if you had the baby, you'd be tied down for the next ten or fifteen years just trying to feed it and send it to school. And as I said, children do better when they have two parents."

"Did you read about that child in New York? How it was beaten and abused?"

"Children are beaten and abused who are living with their own parents. Being adopted is no more dangerous than being a—a natural child."

We drove a few miles. Then he said, "Feeling the way you did, I'm surprised you didn't put up a fight to keep him."

"Are you? With everybody saying the same thing you are, 'It would be better if he had two parents'?"

We drove some more.

"Can we talk about what happened between us without your going into orbit?" he asked.

"All right."

"I liked you. I really did. You seemed shy, not like a lot of the other girls in school. I guess I liked it because I felt shy, too. Half the time, the other girls scared me."

I said slowly, "That's why I liked you. The boys over here, I wasn't used to them. I'd been abroad since I was eleven, and when they—the boys—came on strong, trying to . . . well, grope me in the backseat of a car, I hated it and I didn't know how to handle it."

We drove on for a while. As we approached some houses Alan said, "We're getting to that town you mentioned. "Where's the school?"

I told him how to get there. He slowed the car a good hundred yards from there and put on the brake. "Let me ask you some questions. Did you sign papers when you gave your child up?"

"Of course."

"Did the papers say you gave over all rights with a promise never to try and get in touch?"

A familiar jab went through me. I didn't have to be reminded of that awful moment when I believed I had no choice but to sign them. "Yes."

"Then you know that legally we won't have a leg to stand on, don't you?"

I knew. "Yes," I said. And later I realized it was at that moment that my hope finally died.

— 10 —

We went into the school and rang the bell. I didn't recognize the girl who opened the door. I asked for Miss Gaitskill and gave my name.

"Claudia Ransom?" she said, and giggled a little.

"What's so funny?" Alan said.

She stopped giggling. "Nothing. Wait in here. I'll tell Miss Gaitskill you're here."

We were shown into what had always been called the VIP room, which simply meant it was where important visitors were shown.

"I should have waited," I said miserably. The sight of the school, the familiar outside, which looked so friendly in a New England sort of way, was filling me with a sense of black despair.

In a few minutes Miss Gaitskill came in. Somehow I had been hoping that she was kinder than I remembered. But her face was still rigid and her mouth narrow.

"Well, Claudia, in a way I'm glad that you've had the courage to come here yourself, instead of . . . of manipulating people into making those bogus phone calls, so you could get information which you know you're not allowed to have.''

It wasn't an auspicious beginning.

I opened my mouth, but Alan spoke. "If Claudia has been getting people to call—and you don't know that's true—then it's because she has an entirely understandable desire to know that her child is well placed with good people, and is both happy and well.''

Miss Gaitskill seemed to draw up her flat chest as she took a breath. "Claudia knows perfectly well that I have dedicated my life to making sure that children born out of wedlock have as good a chance at a happy and fulfilling life as any others.''

"If you're entirely certain of yourself in that," Alan said, "then why won't you at least let Claudia find out who has her child and go and satisfy herself?''

"And what about my assurances to the adoptive parents? That the child they have gone to all the trouble and expense of adopting is their own just as much as though it had been born to them? That they wouldn't be harassed by the mother, or the father, in any way, for the simple reason that the details of the adoption would be and would remain totally confidential?''

I interrupted. "But how can you be sure that they're treating my baby all right? Haven't you read about that little girl in New York who was adopted through—through some private arrangement? How she was killed—''

"Please keep your voice down, Claudia. You and your entirely illicit attempts to get details from my staff and from others here is already well known.''

I knew then why the girl at the door had giggled.

"Claudia has a right to express herself any way she

105

wants to. The rights aren't entirely on your side," Alan said. "And she also has a right to be reassured about—"

"What right, Mr. er—?"

"Huntly," Alan said, "And Claudia's baby is also mine."

"You mean you are the father?"

"Yes. I am."

"Then may I ask why you didn't marry Claudia?"

"I don't think that's your business."

"Isn't it? Claudia comes here to this school, is taken care of throughout her pregnancy and during the birth of her child. She then violates the agreement which she— of her own free will—signed, and you come here and tell me I have no right to ask you questions. Are all the rights on your side? What about my rights, which include my ability to continue this school and to guarantee confidentiality to all who come here wishing to adopt? What about the rights of the children who would otherwise be left to be put in foster homes—or find themselves in the kind of situation that destroys children all over the country: Where there is no guarantee of confidentiality, where birth mothers change their minds and laws are bent? How good is that for children not yet born who will need a home?"

I could see that Alan was a little flustered by all the points Miss Gaitskill was bringing up.

Then, "I'm sure you get something out of this, Miss Gaitskill," he said. "You don't do it for free."

She went white at that. "You or your lawyers or the state are completely free to go through my books at any time. Yes, I charge. How else do you think I can keep this school going? Claudia comes from a moneyed background, but others don't. They still have to be paid for.

And now I'm going to bid you good-bye. If you're not out of this house in five minutes, I will call the local police. Is that clear?''

When we were back out on the street and walking to the car, Alan said regretfully, "I'm afraid I was no help. If anything, I made things worse.''

I agreed with him, he had. But as we got into the car I decided that I wouldn't have done any better.''

"I don't think I would have gotten any further," I said. And then I surprised myself by reopening the car door. "I'm going to go back and try again. I have to.''

Alan opened his door. "I'll go—"

"No," I said quickly. Then: "It's not because of what happened when we were there before. But I've got to let her know how I feel.''

"Lotsa luck," he said, and closed his door.

"I don't know whether she'll see you," the girl said when she opened the door a second time.''

"I'll risk it," I said.

Secretly I was afraid, too, that she wouldn't see me, but I had to try. I must have been in the room seven or eight minutes when the girl appeared. "She said to take you back to her study.''

I followed her back into the hall and to the left, where I knew the principal's study was. Like St. Monica's, the school had an annex where most of the girls lived and which contained the classrooms, but it extended from the back, so it didn't show on the street. Miss Gaitskill's study was in the old main building. I'd always associated it with unpleasant confrontations, so I could feel myself tensing as we approached it.

The room was like Miss Gaitskill—old-fashioned, prim,

and neat. She was sitting sideways on a straight chair in front of an old desk.

"Why are you back here?" she said. "I've told you I won't tell you what you want to know."

"I came back to tell you how I feel about it—how awful and frightened I am when I think that some of the things I read about—not just that one case, but other cases, where children are abused and beaten and . . . and . . . I can't think about anything else." I took a shaky breath and went on. "I'm supposed to be working to get into a good college, but I'm not doing that. I can't study properly. I have horrible dreams and can't sleep. If you'll just let me make sure that my baby's all right, I promise, I promise I'll never bother you or . . . or them again."

"And what if it became known that I had given out the name? Do you think other girls in your situation, other families who want to adopt with some assurance of permanence would feel the same confidence in this school? I know being accountable is not a very fashionable concept now. But you should have thought about all this before you took the step that got you into this, shouldn't you?"

"You don't understand or care, do you?" I said. "It's just all moral virtue and being right to you, isn't it?"

There was a silence. I put my hands up to my face and realized I was crying.

"I suppose that's the way it seems to you, doesn't it?" She leaned over and took a small picture I hadn't noticed from the wall near her desk. "Here."

I took it. It was just a snapshot of a girl holding a baby. I couldn't really see the girl's face, because her hair was falling forward as she looked down at the baby.

"That was my daughter, Cecily, and her child. Like your baby, it was born out of wedlock. I didn't even know about it until it was all over. She was away at college. She gave the child for adoption to some people she met there. They weren't very . . . very reliable. They resold the child to some people on another continent. She tried and tried to find out where. She never found out. After two years of trying, she killed herself."

After a minute I said, "That's horrible. I'm sorry. But you must understand how I feel, then?"

"I do, even though you think I don't. I know where your baby is and I know it is well and happy and being loved and looked after, but the whole purpose of my school would be gone if it got around that people who trusted me found I gave in under pressure to birth mothers with second thoughts. It was because of my daughter, and in memory of her that I swore to establish a place where mothers could be absolutely sure that their children would be placed with good people, and they would be checked on from time to time."

"Have you checked on my baby?"

"Yes. He's very well, very healthy and very well taken care of. And the people who have him are good and loving."

"Why didn't you tell me this sooner? Instead of just going on and on about what's right and duty and so on?"

"You sound the way my daughter used to." Her voice seemed funny. I walked around to where I could see her full face instead of just a piece of it. I saw then the marks of the tears on her cheek. And she looked old and tired. Her faded blue eyes stared back at me.

"The trouble probably is that I was middle-aged when

109

I had my daughter. She could have been my granddaughter. She used to accuse me, too, about being full of talk about morality and duty."

I'd met plenty of my friends' grandmothers who seemed a lot younger in attitude than Miss Gaitskill . . . Miss Gaitskill. It took me a minute to take that in.

"But we call you Miss Gaitskill. Weren't you married?"

"Oh yes. But he—my husband—left me shortly afterward and remarried. I took back my maiden name."

"Do you think your daughter killed herself because of . . . well, because you're so morally strict?" I realized how cruel it sounded, but I didn't care.

"Do you think I haven't wondered about that?" She looked at me. "She had . . . she had certain serious emotional problems, and was under medical care many years of her life. From time to time she would stop taking her medicine. . . . In answer to your question, I don't know." She got up. "The funny part is, you sometimes remind me of her—at least in appearance. Which is perhaps why I'm upset now. But despite everything, I'm not going to do as you ask. I learned only two weeks ago that your baby is well and happy. If you can't trust me over his welfare, then there's nothing I can do. I'm sorry you think I'm a moral prude. But that's the way I am and I have to accept it, just as someday you will have to accept the way you are, even if you don't particularly like it. And now, this has been as tiring for me as it has been for you. And I'm a lot older."

"It's because of her—your daughter—that you started this place?"

"Yes. I wanted a place where girls could be absolutely sure their children would be happily adopted."

"What would you do if you found they weren't—I mean the parents weren't doing as they promised?"

"I have set up the legal means to take the child back."

We stood there, she and I. I knew that was as far as I could get. "Good-bye," I said.

I was almost at the door when she said, "Are you and that young man going to marry?"

I turned. "He's married." I didn't add that he was trying to get out of it.

"I see. On the whole, I'm glad. You're a strong girl, Claudia, and I don't think he'd make you happy. You'd do better with somebody who is as strong-willed, some would say pig-headed, as you."

"Where do you want me to take you?" Alan said as we drove toward the turnpike.

"To the bus terminal, I guess."

"You've decided to go back home?"

"What else can I do?"

"Can you think of anyone else who was at the school there who might help you?"

"Only one of the teachers, a Prunella Halsey. She was the person I was trying to reach when I called from home."

"What a name! I take it she was more sympathetic?"

"Yes. I guess that's why she was canned."

"And you don't know where she is now?"

"No. And Trudy Shannon, the girl in Boston I told you about, didn't know either."

We drove for quite a while without saying anything, then Alan asked, "What are you going to do now?"

"I just told you, I don't know."

111

"No, I mean what are you going to do with your life?"

I thought in a brief flash of Miss Gaitskill's daughter, who killed herself. For a second I was sure I knew how she felt, and then I realized I didn't, because I couldn't really imagine killing myself.

"Miss Gaitskill's daughter killed herself because she lost track of her baby," I said, and I told Alan what the principal had told me.

"I can see why she considers not breaking confidence a sort of sacred trust." He glanced sideways at me. "But I don't really worry about your doing likewise. I know you've had a blow, but you're pretty tough."

"Thanks."

"In the long run, it's a useful quality. And I'm afraid it's one I don't have enough of."

Before talking to Miss Gaitskill I'd have contradicted that loudly. Now, I knew she—and he—were right. Weird, I thought. I'd spent so many weeks crying because Alan was such a rotten jerk, not telling me about his wife, not offering to divorce her. "Did you or your wife actually leave?" I asked.

He didn't answer for a moment, then, "As a matter of fact, it was Susan."

A week ago, even two days ago, I thought, I'd have sent up rockets of delight. Now I didn't care. Somehow that was almost as terrible as not finding out about my baby.

"Are you all right?" he asked.

"Fine," I said.

Going back to school wasn't easy. For one thing, I'd always felt like Ms. Outsider. Only then I had a big

112

secret to account for it. Now I still had the secret, but it was different. Before, I knew that it was still open, not yet finished in my mind. Now it was finished.

Uncle James and Aunt Mary, whom I'd called from the bus terminal in Vermont, met me at the one in New York and then drove me back home. I sat in the car, braced for their comments. But after asking about the outcome, they didn't say anything. Finally I said, "I'm sorry I ran away after you'd offered to help. But—I didn't think anything would have made her tell."

"No, from what you've told us, you're probably right," Uncle James said.

"We're just sorry you had to go through it all," Aunt Mary said from the backseat. She put her hand on my shoulder. Briefly I touched it.

"Thanks," I said, and braced myself for more statements of regret. But there weren't any. We drove in silence for some miles. Then they started chatting about a party they'd been to.

I said, interrupting, "I met the father of my baby, Alan Huntly, in Vermont."

"Were you glad to see him?" Aunt Mary asked.

"Yes. Although I wanted to kill him—at first. I told him about the baby and why I was there, so he drove me to the town where the school is. And he went in to talk to the principal with me."

Uncle James cleared his throat. "Are you still angry at him?"

I thought about this for a few minutes. "A little. But not the way I was."

There was another silence. Then Uncle James said,

113

"Can you tell us a little about him? Or would you rather not?"

They were being so tactful and considerate that I found I suddenly wanted to scream, Stop walking on eggshells! I won't break! But I knew I couldn't.

"He's older. About twenty-eight or nine. He was working on his doctorate at the university at home. I met him in the library. I wasn't getting along with the other kids in my class. All they wanted to do was hang out . . . and I guess I didn't know how to do that. I mean, things weren't like they were in France. There, people—kids—went home more. Anyway, I'd go to the library, and noticed him. We got to talking. He wasn't like the others. He says now he felt shy. I just thought he wasn't like what I called the football hearties—you know, the kind of boys who get you into the back of a car and seemed to have six pairs of hands."

"But I take it the shy Alan succeeded where the oafs failed."

I sighed. "Yes. We went back to his apartment and he gave me something to drink."

"Was he planning—er—mischief?" Uncle James asked.

"He said he wasn't. Anyway, it was strong, and—well, you know what happened. Then I didn't see him anymore. When I discovered I was pregnant, and tried to find him, I was told he had gone abroad. I was also told he was married."

"Less and less creditable," Aunt Mary said. "Surely he ought to know what could happen to him—er—interfering with the morals of a minor. I wonder if he thought of that."

"He says he didn't open my mouth and force the liquor down."

114

"He probably didn't. But since you were—what, sixteen?—no court would take such a lenient view of it."

The thought of making Alan suffer would once have been unbearably attractive. At the moment, I couldn't get excited about it.

"By the way," Aunt Mary said, "some motel in Boston called and asked if it was your backpack they were holding. I guess they'd read about you in the paper. Anyway, they sent it on to us and I put it in your room."

As we got back near the house, I said rather drearily, "I'm going to have to make up lost classes and grades."

Aunt Mary said, "We were wondering if you'd rather let it all go until after Christmas, then start afresh in another school, a boarding school."

I hesitated. "Do people here know?"

There was silence, then Aunt Mary said, "I'm not sure. I haven't, to my knowledge, let any cat out of the bag, and your uncle says he didn't either. But I have heard rumors of whispers that some people have been making inspired guessing."

"Speaking of cats," Uncle James said. "Samantha will be glad to see you."

"Is she all right?"

"Yes. But we kept her in your room when we were out because she cried a lot and kept mewing around our feet as though she were looking for you, and we didn't want her to wander onto the road."

"Thanks," I said. "And I'm sorry I—well—acted like I thought you wouldn't feed her."

"Think about the school bit and let us know. We have

ties to a nice school not too far from here. They'd take you, I'm sure."

We drove up to the house and I got out. I don't know what I expected to feel, maybe as though something were over and something else beginning.

But I didn't feel anything at all. Absolutely nothing. Then I heard a familiar mewing. There, her paws against the window, yelling her head off, was Samantha.

I started to run toward the house.

— 11 —

Nobody said anything at school, which made me pretty sure they knew at least something of what had happened. And nobody came near me, until at the end of an English class Miss Strickland asked me to stay behind.

When the others had gone, she said, "You've been away. Your uncle and aunt tried to make people think you were visiting one of your parents temporarily in New York. But I think everyone was pretty well aware that that wasn't the case. You ran away, didn't you?"

"Yes."

"Can you tell me what happened?"

"All right." I was starting to talk, when somebody came into the class with a note for her.

"We'd better finish this in my apartment. Can you come there after school?"

"I have extra lab today, but I could come tomorrow."

"All right. Around four?"

It was later that afternoon that I ran into Jeff Talbot in the hall. I suddenly remembered pushing him in the fountain and started to laugh.

He stopped. "Something funny?" He wasn't smiling.

"No. I'm sorry I pushed you in the fountain."

"Just out of curiosity, why did you?"

"You came on so strong, putting your hand on my leg and stuff like that."

There was a pause. Then: "From the stories going around, you should be used to that. You're not exactly the lily-white virgin you're pretending to be. Boys have done a lot more than just put a hand on you!"

I was suddenly aware of a small crowd around us. More than anything I wanted to run. But I had run and run and run, and got nowhere.

"Not boys, Jeff. A boy. A doctoral student who seemed as shy as I felt. Only trusting him, I went to his apartment and he gave me something to drink—I don't mean a drug or anything. Just a regular drink. But I wasn't used to it. We had sex. I had a baby which was put up for adoption. That has been my experience of sex. Period. And it was enough." And I walked away.

I kept walking until I got to the place where my bicycle (which miraculously was not stolen from the bus terminal) was tied. I was about to go home when I thought about the lab I was supposed to go to. For a long moment I stood there beside the bike. Some of the other kids turned around and looked at me as they passed. I stared back. Then I shoved the bike back in the stand and went to the lab.

The next afternoon at four o'clock I went to Miss Strickland's apartment.

"Come in," she said when I rang the bell, and stepped back from the door.

This time as I went into the living room I saw things I hadn't seen before—mainly silver cups.

"You got those riding?" I asked.

"Yes, a long time ago."

I walked over and looked at the cups. "Were these here the other day? I don't remember seeing them. Maybe I wasn't up to remembering much that day."

"You were pretty upset," Miss Strickland said. "Come sit down." When I had sat down on the sofa opposite her she said, "Did you succeed in finding out what you wanted?"

I shook my head. "No. She—Miss Gaitskill— wouldn't tell me where my baby was. She said . . . she said she'd founded the school so that adopting parents could be absolutely sure no—no birth mothers would find out where their children were and come after them."

There was a silence. "Have you come to accept that?" Miss Strickland asked.

I shrugged. "I don't have any choice." I paused. "I called Alan, the baby's father, when I was in Vermont. He lives there. He drove me to the school."

"Does he seem quite the villain he was before?"

"I guess not. But I still think it was a rotten thing to do—to have an affair with me and not tell me he was married."

"I agree it wasn't an attractive or . . . or considerate thing to do. So what happens now?"

"Everybody's asking me that, and I don't know. Apart from trying to get into a good college."

"What year are you trying for? Not next year, I shouldn't think. Not if you want to get into a top one."

"But I hate the idea of going to school another year. I

119

really hate it!'' Until I said that, I hadn't realized how much I did hate it.

"Do you think you could get into a decent college without another year? There are such things as transcripts and SATs, and even if you sailed past those, your application should be in by January, or February at the latest.''

"I don't know why all these things have to happen to me," I said glumly.

"Why not to you?"

I looked at her and she looked back. "I've always hated this 'why me?' attitude," she said, "as though some deity had arbitrarily decided you, and not six dozen others, should be given some extra dose of ill fate.''

"It happens!''

"Yes, but not as often as the professional self-pitiers would have you believe. Two people can be hit with the same crushing and debilitating disease, yet one will somehow struggle and fight through it, while the other just refuses to accept reality and won't cope with it. Yet it's always the one who isn't trying who moans 'why me?' "

Suddenly I was so angry I didn't know what to do. I thought my anger, formerly directed at Alan Huntly and Miss Gaitskill, had died. It hadn't. I got up. "That's a cruel, unsympathetic thing to say.''

"Why is it, Claudia? A man, admittedly a not very responsible man, gets you pregnant and you're awash in self-pity! As though you yourself had nothing to do with it.''

"I can't even find out how my baby is!''

"You've been assured again and again that your baby is in good condition and well taken care of."

"How do I know she's telling the truth?"

"Why do you have so much investment in believing the worst? So you can feel sorry for yourself?"

I picked up my bookbag and started out.

"Just a minute, Claudia." Miss Strickland got up and came to the door where I was. "Despite what you think, I'm not trying to be cruel. I just want you to get on with your life. You have a lot of talent. I know you write well and I'm told by the art teacher that you have ability there. She even said you were thinking of doing a children's book—both the writing and the illustration. So why don't you? You can do a lot with yourself if you just—well, try! But running around and accusing everybody else of being the cause of your misery isn't the way to do it."

"How do you know? You've never had a baby!"

"What makes you so sure?"

For a moment I was stopped. "That's just a dodge, a game. I'm leaving!"

I stormed out of the apartment. My rage had come out of nowhere. Before that I'd been feeling . . . what? Numb, like everything was gray.

As I passed the fountain in the mall I glanced at it, remembering Jeff's face as I pushed him in. But there was nobody sitting on the side now.

I don't know what happened to me after that. The days, and then after a while the weeks, passed slowly by. My parents, who had planned coming back to the States for either Thanksgiving or Christmas, evidently decided I was doing well enough so that they didn't have to.

I went to school, handed in homework—occasionally, when I felt like it, and stared out the window in class, daydreaming. I knew my grades were going down, but I also didn't care. And I was curious to see if anyone at school would call me on the mat about it. They didn't. So I cut class more often and more frequently didn't bother with the homework.

And then one day Uncle James said at dinner, taking some letters out of his pocket and putting them on the table, "You've been through a lot, Claudia, I know, but are you sure flunking out of school is the best way to go? Because if you don't change course, that's what you're going to do."

I shrugged. "I don't care. I'm not interested in being a scholar."

"I'm not sorry to hear that. I've never thought of you as a permanent long-time denizen of the ivory tower. Still, a degree is an advantage, and if you don't buckle down, Winsocki, buckle down, you're not even going to pass your junior year in high school, let alone get into a college."

I knew I should care, but I didn't. So I didn't say anything.

"If your school didn't cost anything, I wouldn't, maybe, feel so strongly about it. But it's private and costs quite a lot, and I don't think your parents are that rich so that you needn't care."

"Mother makes a lot of money in her law practice."

"Maybe so. But she isn't practicing law this year, and I'd be willing to bet what she's getting overseas is a lot of kudos and credit, not a lot of money."

I shrugged. "She and Dad wanted me to come to this school. I didn't care. I'd just as soon have gone to a public one."

"Whom are you angry at now?" Aunt Mary said.

"I'm not angry at anyone," I said, and knew as I spoke that it was a lie. The funny part was, I really wasn't that sure who I was angry at now, unless it was everyone. Always before, whenever I felt my anger like a hot balloon inside me, I knew who I was angry at. The anger would burn extra hot whenever I thought about him or her. But now all I felt was nothing. Just blah and not like doing anything the school or anybody else wanted me to.

One day I took out the children's book I had been tinkering with. It had been about a girl who had set out to find the pony that had been stolen from her. But without even thinking about it, the girl became a boy, a boy of about ten, who, with his cat, went to find the woman who was his mother, but who had always been kept from him. What I liked doing more than the actual story were the illustrations, which I did in colored crayons. The path through the forest got more and more frightening. Faces of witches and monsters appeared between the branches of the trees. The cat, who looked very like Samantha, walked close to the little boy.

"Did you see yourself, Samantha?" I said, and showed her the picture.

She rolled over on her back and showed her furry stomach. Thanksgiving came and went. We celebrated Thanksgiving dinner at Aunt Mary's club. Afterwards I went to the kitchen and begged some scraps for Samantha, who gobbled them up, especially the dark meat.

A week or so later the principal sent for me.

"Claudia, I've been looking at your grades. Unless you improve them considerably, you're not going to pass the year. Yet Miss Strickland tells me you don't even want to complete your senior year before applying to college. You couldn't possibly get in anywhere that you'd want to go, unless you change course radically."

I stared back at her and wondered if she'd ever had a baby or a boyfriend.

"Well," she said.

"I don't care," I said, and as I said it felt a great thrust of satisfaction.

"I see. Well, I'll have to write your parents."

"All right."

She sat there looking at me and I stared back. I wondered about the jacket I'd given the boy in my book, whether it shouldn't have been a duller color. It didn't do to give him too lively an appearance at this point in the story.

"Claudia, what are you thinking about now—this minute?"

"Nothing," I said. I wasn't about to talk about my boy on his search.

She sighed. "All right. You can go now."

I cut the next class, which happened to be Miss Strickland's, and went instead to the art shop in the mall, where I thought I could find a special sort of light brown crayon.

As I was picking out the right color crayon, I wondered what my baby was going to get for Christmas. But I didn't want to think about that, because I found that when I thought about him, my heart would speed up and I'd get a funny breathless feeling. And since I'd never be able to

124

know where he was, there was no point in thinking about him anyway.

It was strange, I didn't talk to anyone these days. And nobody at school talked to me. I decided I'd play a game: I'd pretend that there was no one at school except me. That everyone had left except me.

It was fun, really. I'd walk along the halls telling myself that all those figures I thought were the other kids and the teachers were really not there—just images that would one day disappear. When a teacher called on me in class, I'd pretend I hadn't heard. I decided when I finished the book I was working on, I'd do another about a girl who put her cat in a basket, put the basket up in front of her when she rode her horse, and took off to a country where there were no people. . . .

"Claudia!" The voice came like a cannon shot near my ear. I jumped and turned.

It was Jeff. I told myself he wasn't really there.

He took my arm in his hand. "Listen," he said, "your uncle—" I yanked my arm loose. "Don't touch me," I yelled. Then I ran down the hall and out into the school yard.

It was Uncle James whom I saw suddenly, walking slowly toward me from his car parked in the street.

"Claudia, Claudia," he said. His voice was gentle. "Don't run away. I have some . . . some sad news for you."

There was something in his voice that frightened me.

When he got nearer and I saw his face, I knew something awful had happened. "What—what happened?"

"Samantha—she wandered out into the road. I don't think she suffered. But—she's dead, Claudia. I took her to the vet, but—there's nothing he can do."

I stared at him, and then out of my mouth came a scream. I screamed and screamed. "No, no, no!"

His arms were around me and he was holding me and saying, "I'm sorry! I'm so sorry, Claudia."

"You let her out," I screamed. "It's your fault."

"No, we didn't, truly—"

"You must have! I always close my door."

"I'm afraid today you left it open. Come along, I'm taking you back to the house."

I don't remember the ride back. I cried as I had never cried before. "Why is God doing this to me?" I said.

"I really don't think God has anything to do with it."

"I didn't leave my door open. I never leave my door open." But as I said it I knew it was true. I could remember walking out the door and knowing, as I went down the stairs, that I had left something undone.

I was allowed to bury Samantha in the garden under a tree. I put up a little plaque, saying Samantha, Truly Beloved.

I was surprised to receive some letters from some of the kids in school saying they were sorry. One from Jeff said his favorite dog, a Labrador, had died the year before, and he still thought about him all the time.

"Do you want to go to school?" Aunt Mary said. "If you don't, you can stay home until after New Year's."

I almost accepted, when I realized that I'd be at home, and there'd be no Samantha.

"No," I said. "I'd rather go to school."

Two weeks before Christmas the phone rang one night. "It's for you," Uncle James said, coming into the room. He paused. "It's Alan Huntly."

A jab of pain went through me. I thought about refusing to talk to him, but I didn't even have the energy for that. I went into the hall and picked up the phone. "Alan?"

"Claudia, I've found where your—where our baby is."

— 12 —

For a moment the words had no meaning, then I almost shouted, "Where?"

"You remember the teacher you kept trying to find, Prunella Halsey? I ran into her in a conference of English teachers. I knew there couldn't be too many Prunella Halseys, so I was pretty sure it had to be yours. I got to talking to her and finally told her who I was. Claudia, the baby was adopted by people she knows and sees all the time, people who live near Boston."

"Oh, Alan!" I was crying so much I could hardly talk. "Is he—is he all right?"

"He's fine, flourishing. Listen, I told her about how hard you tried to find her, and about our going to see the principal of that school. She told me to tell you, if you want to know from her that the baby's okay, you can call her. I'll give you the number." And he read a number over the phone. "And Claudia, if you're going to see the baby, I'd like to see him, too. So please call me. I'm at—" He read another number.

After we'd hung up I sat there, still crying. Uncle James came out and said, "What did he have to say?"

"He ran into Miss Halsey, the teacher I liked, at an English teachers' conference. He told her about my wanting to find the baby to make sure he was all right, and she said he was adopted by friends of hers, that she sees them all the time, and he's fine. He gave me her number to call."

It was weird. At long last I had got what I had searched for with so much trouble, and all I could do was cry.

"Then you'd better call her, hadn't you?"

My hand shook so much, I had to make two efforts at dialing. Finally I heard it ring.

Somebody answered the phone by saying Something College.

"I'd like to speak to Miss Halsey," I said. "Miss Prunella Halsey."

When she came on the phone, I blurted out who I was and about Alan's phone call.

"Yes, he told me. I'm sorry you've had such a bad time, Claudia, but your baby is really fine. They're nice people who've adopted him. The father is a teacher in the college here and they're making wonderful parents. I suppose strictly speaking, I shouldn't be telling you this, but nothing Alan said led me to think that you wanted to take him back. Is that true?"

The day before, an hour before Alan's phone call, I'd have sworn that my answer would have been yes. I did want to take him back. But now—"It's just that I have to know, without any doubt, that he's okay. I've read so many awful stories about kids being abused, including adopted ones, and I haven't been able to sleep or study—and Miss Gaitskill didn't understand."

"No. She's not as grim as she makes out or people think, but she's also rather rigid."

129

"Did she fire you?" I asked. "Nobody knew where you'd gone."

Miss Halsey laughed. "We fired each other. I came to understand some of her motivation, but I'll admit, she was pretty unbending and I defied her rather a lot."

"She told me about her daughter."

"I'm surprised she'd do that. You must have got through to her."

There was then a silence. Finally Miss Halsey said, "I suppose you want to see your baby, only he isn't really your baby now, you know. He has a set of parents that love him very much and would be desperately unhappy if you tried to take him away."

"I know. I don't want to take him away, but if I could just see him."

She sighed. "All right. Give me your telephone number."

I stayed near the phone until it rang about an hour and a half later.

Miss Halsey said, "Understandably, they're not happy with the idea of your coming here, but I tried to explain. So they said you could come to their house Saturday afternoon around two. You can come up to Boston on the shuttle. Alan can meet you and drive you here."

"All right. Thank you. Thank you."

Uncle James and Aunt Mary weren't awfully happy, either. "I can't help feeling it's a mistake," Aunt Mary said. "But it's obviously what you want."

I called Alan back, and he said he'd call for me at Logan Airport at twelve-thirty.

* * *

Before I left on Saturday, I went out and put a flower from the living room on Samantha's grave. "It was my fault," I said to her as I stood there. "I wasn't thinking . . . I didn't think about anything but my baby and I forgot to close the door. I'm sorry! I miss you!" Saying it, admitting it, was hard, but I felt oddly relieved.

Uncle James and Aunt Mary drove me to the airport. Alan met me in Boston and drove me to the address Miss Halsey had given. Before going to the house, we stopped and had some lunch. Then we got back in the car.

Alan stopped a little short of the address. "Are you going to be all right, doing this?" he asked.

"Yes."

He stared at me for a minute or two. "I hope to God I did the right thing about setting this in motion—right for you, for the baby and for the parents."

I thought about the word *parents* that didn't refer to Alan and me. "I hope so too."

Then we got out and walked to the house, a white clapboard affair behind a small green lawn. We had driven around the college before reaching there, and knew it was only a block or two away.

The air was crisp and cold, and the trees, all bare except for the evergreens, held naked brown limbs up to the sky.

We rang the bell. A woman somewhere in her thirties opened the door. She had brown eyes and looked anxious. But she smiled. "Claudia Ransom?"

"Yes. And this is Alan Huntly."

She stepped back. "Come in. Peter is in the living room."

I had secretly named him Alex, but his name was really Peter.

There was a playpen in the living room. A baby in a

red corduroy one-piece suit was sitting inside. Beside him, batting at a toy strung across the top of the pen, was a puppy. Obviously the baby and the puppy got along well together.

I stood there and looked at my baby. He had blue eyes like both Alan and me and dark blond straight hair. He was now ten months and two days.

"Hi, Peter," I said.

He gurgled, pulled the puppy's ear and then laughed.

"Hi, Peter," Alan said, and walked over to the other side.

I looked at Peter playing with the puppy for a while. At one point the puppy fell over on its back. Peter laughed and then bent over and hugged it. A man came in and stood beside his wife. He was older than Alan, sort of stocky, with a short beard, and was very kind looking. He squatted down and pushed a finger at Peter, who threw up his arms and tried to hug the man's hand and giggled some more.

"He looks very happy," I said. I knew in my insides that this was a good home for Peter, that he would be happy and loved here. Still, it was hard to turn around and go.

"Good-bye Peter," I said at the door. He looked at me once, but went back to the puppy.

"Thanks," I said to the parents. "Thanks a lot. I won't bother you again. I promise."

Alan drove me home. "What are you going to do?" he asked as we approached the house.

"I'm going to go to college, or maybe art school."

"But you're a junior, aren't you?"

"Yes, but if there's a way I can manage, I'm not going to spend another year here in school."

"If you really make up your mind to, and your grades are good, you might be able to take the SATs and apply for early admission to college."

"My grades have been absolutely lousy for the past weeks. I can't explain it, exactly, but nothing made any sense. I cut class and didn't bother to work. I wish now I hadn't, but I did."

"You could go abroad for a year, maybe at a special school. Or you could work like hell here. Or you could do a special project of some kind, with a guidance teacher."

I thought of my book. We drove up to the house.

"Samantha died," I said.

"Your cat?"

"Yes. I was in my phase of not paying attention to anything and left the door to my room open. She got out and onto the street and was killed."

"You know you can't take responsibility for everything that goes wrong. Couldn't she have gotten out anyway? Out a window? Onto the limb of a tree or something?"

I sat there in the car, the tears rolling down my cheeks. Alan leaned over. "Listen, Claudia, you don't realize it now, but your life is just beginning. You're bright and quick and attractive. Don't—don't be down on yourself."

I gave him a watery smile. "Okay. Thanks."

I got out of the car and stuck my head back through the window. "Good-bye. You have a good life, too."

"I'll try." He waved and drove off.

I unlocked the front door and went in. Normally Uncle James and Aunt Mary would have eaten by now, but I wasn't sure whether they had. I switched on the hall light and then nearly fell over something.

There was a loud squawk. Looking up at me was a ginger kitten.

"Who's that?" I asked as Uncle James came from the living room.

"That's Jamesie. He arrived in a carrier with your name on it. Here's the note that came with it."

I opened the envelope. "Jamesie needs a home. I heard about Samantha. J. is just a mutt, but I thought maybe you'd take him. I'll call you over the weekend."

It was signed "Jeff."

Jamesie made a dart at my foot, then went under the hall chair. After a minute I squatted down and stuck out my finger. Jamesie licked it, then gave it a gentle bite.

"Everything all right?" Aunt Mary asked, coming out of the living room.

"Yes."

"What are you going to do now?" Uncle James said. "That is, besides having dinner, which we've kept until you got here."

Jamesie rubbed against my leg. If I put on an extra push, I thought, I might be able to get into a college next fall. There had to be ways of doing it, because I'd known kids who had. And maybe, after dinner, I'd call Jeff and tell him how Jamesie was getting on.

I rubbed Jamesie between his ears and straightened up. "Get on with my life, I guess."

About the Author

Isabelle Holland, the daughter of an American diplomatic officer, was born in Basel, Switzerland. After living in several countries, she moved to the United States to finish college. She spent a number of years in publishing before turning to writing as a career. In addition to her numerous young adult books, Ms. Holland writes adult mysteries. She lives in New York City.

MORE POPULAR THAN EVER

Isabelle Holland

11/90   TAF-117